THE MOON WILL FOREVER BE A DISTANT LOVE

THE MOON WILL FOREVER BE A DISTANT LOVE

Luis Humberto Crosthwaite

———— TRANSLATED BY ————

Debbie Nathan & Willivaldo Delgadillo

 CINCO PUNTOS PRESS ▸ EL PASO TEXAS

Originally published in Mexico in 1994 as *La luna siempre será un difícil amor* by Ediciones Corunda.

FIRST EDITION

Library of Congress Cataloging-in-Publication Data

    Crosthwaite, Luis Humberto, 1962-
        [Luna siempre será un dificíl amor. English]
        The moon will forever be a distant love / by Luis Humberto
           Crosthwaite; translated by Debbie Nathan and Willivaldo
           Delgadillo.
              p.   cm.
        ISBN 0-938317-31-8 (pbk.)
        1. Balboa, Vasco Núñez de, 1475-1519—Fiction. I. Nathan,
           Debbie. II. Delgadillo, Willivaldo, 1960-. III. Title.
    PQ7298.13.R67L8613   1997
    863—dc21
                                   97-26920
                                   CIP

Cover art, cover and book design by Vicki Trego Hill of El Paso, Texas.

This book is funded in part by
generous support from

FIDEICOMISO PARA LA CULTURA MEXICO/USA

THE ROCKEFELLER FOUNDATION ♦ FUNDACION CULTURAL BANCOMER
FONDO NACIONAL PARA LA CULTURA Y LAS ARTES

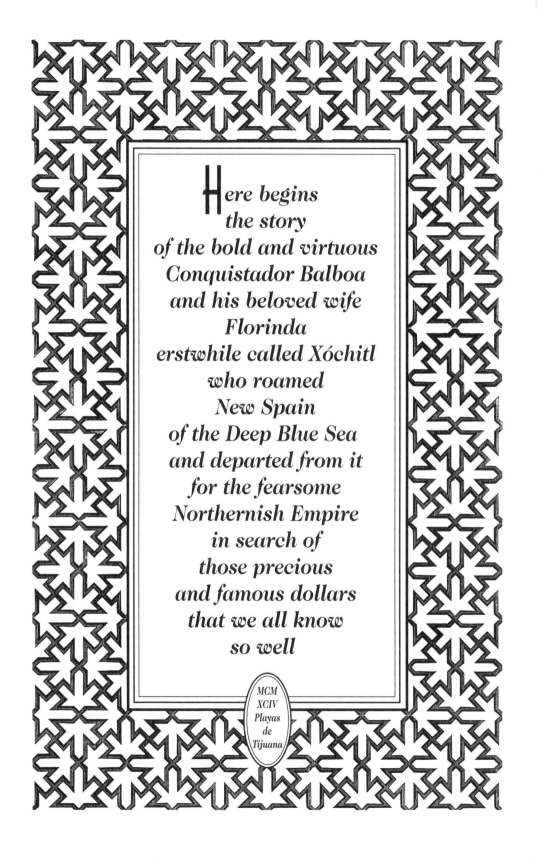

Here begins
the story
of the bold and virtuous
Conquistador Balboa
and his beloved wife
Florinda
erstwhile called Xóchitl
who roamed
New Spain
of the Deep Blue Sea
and departed from it
for the fearsome
Northernish Empire
in search of
those precious
and famous dollars
that we all know
so well

MCM
XCIV
Playas
de
Tijuana

And she says: Hansel, you're really bringing me down
And he says: Gretel, you can really be a bitch
He says: I've wasted my life on our stupid legend
When my one and only love
was the wicked witch.

—LAURIE ANDERSON
  The Dream Before

PART ONE

In Which Love Emerges, as Well as Fabada

*like a knight from some old-fashioned book
I have saved all my ribbons for thee*

—Leonard Cohen

The Conquest

———

AMID THE MARKETS AND CANALS
of the great city of Mexicco-Tenochtitlan,
smack on the corner where nowadays Dolores Street
runs past the Chinese restaurants and umbrella stores,
Conquistador Balboa is in a rush to run an errand
for the Marquis, and the Indian girl Florinda
is walking to the flea market. By pure chance
they bump into each other and find themselves
face to face. Their eyes meet
for an instant,

▼

and thus, inevitably,
the following tale begins:

The Emergence of Love and Other Things

WHEN CONQUISTADOR BALBOA meets the Indian girl Florinda, his young Spaniard's heart wants to leap from its armor and dives blissfully beneath the waters of Lake Texcoco. The metal hinges of his armor squeak an amorous song that ordinary lubricants could hardly silence. The Conquistador is unable to speak. Not even a "Good Afternoon" comes out of his Spaniard's mouth. Not even "Hot enough for you?" or "Nice day, huh?" much less an invitation for lunch.

When the Indian Florinda meets Conquistador Balboa, her heart does a pirouette. But she hides it under her simple dress adorned with flowers and artifice. She smiles slightly at the poor, naive conquistador's nervousness, but feigns total indifference.

No one can convince her that Balboa is Mr. Right. Florinda could never give her love to just anybody. He must have something positive and productive about him. No doubt about it, this one's got class, in his two-cornered helmet with its white feathers. And his beard makes him look so attractive, so serious. When he smiles he's like the gods all together on Sunday.

But all that is secondary.

What's important is whether he's willing to help her realize her full potential: like if she wants to go to school, improve herself, work, etc.

She doesn't want a domineering, drunken husband like her father.

Florinda figured all this out when she was fifteen, but what's terrible is that two years have already gone by, yet her head still doesn't always rule over her heart.

Conquistador Balboa is the closest thing you can get to a cinema heart throb. This fact presses inside her body with force and tenderness, with enthusiasm and passion.

For his part, poor naive Balboa can't think of anything unless it's about Love love. Not Valentine-hearts-and-chocolate-bar love, but Love love. Not just-give-me-a-little-kiss-and- I'll-love-you-forever love, or Hey-baby-come-here-let's-get-it-on love. No. The kind of love that sways decisions, that tortures madmen, that kicks dogs. LOVE love.

The young conquistador doesn't understand his feelings. He thinks they're like the wind that moves ships, or the weather that brings thunder and lightening. It's not easy to explain.

Florinda has the most delicate face. And long hair—black and straight. How he would like to tell her about his adventures while she was getting dressed, combing her hair or washing up. In this cold world of conquered lands and corrupt officials, Florinda is virgin territory. His island, his continent, his voyage 'round the world. With her, he has no need to go down in History, because History has not yet been discovered. And Florinda is here, in the New World, to discover it by his side.

The young Indian girl, almost a child, needs something more solid than the shy stare and mumblings of the conquistador. A sign perhaps. Some divine affirmation to confirm that he is her man for life, her partner unto old age. Suddenly, the sign manifests itself as they walk down one of the avenues of the great city.

Balboa is wearing his high boots and she is walking barefoot.

Florinda feels a sharp pain and looks at her red, red blood, spilt all over the ground.

Someone has carelessly thrown out a bunch of broken Coca-Cola and Carta Blanca bottles.

Florinda notes the warm blood of Time pooling at her feet, and feels the arms of her conquistador, lifting her up to carry her to the nearest hospital.

She looks at his heavy breathing and his sweaty, drawn face, sharing her pain. The hospital's white halls open with their strange, hygienic smell. "It's an emergency," Balboa explains to the shift nurse, and she asks for the patient's name and address. "It's an emergency!" he insists, and she inquires about blood type and place of birth. Is it possible that Florinda is Spanish—or at least criolla or mestiza?

"No, of course she's not," the nurse figures as she looks at the girl's dark skin. "It's highly unlikely that a doctor would take a look at her. I doubt any of them will want to."

Florinda, getting weaker by the minute, sees how brave her conquistador is as he fights for her. She understands that yes, there surely must be some love in this tale. Something thriving lasting eternal.

Balboa sneaks another card from his sleeve. He tells the nurse that his boss is the Marquis del Valle. He's not one to try to impress people, but he feels Florinda sinking fast.

The look on the nurse's face grows less hostile. She immediately calls a doctor. Somebody brings a stretcher.

Balboa has to wait.

Time travels on a slow voyage, through a fog, with no safe place to dock.

The hours are insurmountable obstacles, walled cities impossible to breech.

Is the young conquistador going to be sick?

A thousand exploits parade before him in the waiting room: battles, deaths, fetid smells, the Conquest.

Then, making his way through the gun powder, the doctor comes, saying that everything will be just fine. Only a few stitches. A lot of blood lost though. But don't you worry, young man. *Everything* will be just fine.

Getting to Know Florinda

I N THE MORNING, in the lavish room filled with desks and filing cabinets, the bureaucrats (old conquistadors, new dreamers) pull out their stories as though unsheathing marvelous swords.

Amadis, Percival, Tirant, Lancelot—such could be the names of each of the conquistadors who wander around amid the adding machines and the calculators. How much gold? How much adventure? How many beautiful maidens?

Dionisio, a long-haired conquistador, tells his story as he files papers in alphabetical order. His fellow employees gather about him, sitting on the floor or on their desktops to listen to the same old things they've heard before. Dionisio was one of the first conquistadors to arrive. Did they know that? He looked upon the high pyramids, the markets, the water-filled canals that Indians travelled through in canoes. And like the same tired joke told over and over in a barroom, his story evokes the same twitch, the same surprise—it raises people's hair and makes them shiver.

Maglorio, the handless one, is also here. He who accompanied Nuño de Guzmán in his ruthless search for fame and fortune.

Old Artaldo, half blind, hunchbacked, who everyone knows accompanied Cabeza de Vaca, but who refuses to talk about it since he knows there will always be some friend or film maker to tell the story for him.

Rogaciano, the gay conquistador, saw Cuauhtémoc hanging from a tree on the road to Hibueras, his Indian legs gleaming and kicking in the sun.

Gaudencio, the intellectual, who has read Amadís de Gaula seventeen times, and the truth of whose adventures nobody would dare challenge—those adventures with the notable caballero and his son Esplandián, who fiercely fought the Amazons. There is a loyalty among these bureaucrat conquistadors, one hard to find among others in the same trade.

Carilao, with the runny nose, met the unlucky Captain Pedro de Ursúa before his voyage, and (it should be made clear) before calamity and misfortune led to his sad demise.

As for Balboa, his greatest feat was meeting Florinda. She conquered his heart, captivated him with her feminine caress, and made him turn his back on his adventurous nature. All the riches in the world would never mean anything to him now, not even for a moment. But Balboa tries not to say anything. No one would understand. He lets the others speak, and listens to the stories of Maglorio, Artaldo, Rogaciano and Gaudencio, celebrating and cursing as if they were telling these stories in a bar for the first time.

The clock says it's 11 A.M.

Like gossipy secretaries, the bureaucrat conquistadors rush back to their desks and their silence.

The Marquis del Valle, neurotic boss of them all, will soon arrive.

15

A Brief Monologue from the Marquis

NOT LONG AGO, I received an edict from His Holy Catholic Royal Majesty, Don Carlos, in which I am informed of the terrible crisis and times of austerity which the kingdom is experiencing. It hath been said to me, alas to my great sorrow, that as an act of solidarity in facing this crisis, I shall be forced to implement a personnel cut, a gradual elimination of unsatisfactory employees, those who find themselves on the payroll earning a fair wage; but who have not appreciated all that we have done in their behalf. In like manner, thou knowest, my dear Balboa, that soon will be named the first viceroy of New Spain, and that it has been said, it is said and it shall be said, that I'm in the running as one of the top four or five candidates for this illustrious post. It is for this reason, also, that I must assuage any sort of scandal that might arise in my domain. Thou already knowest the ways of the press, Balboa; that it doth not suffer a person to live; that it measureth one's every step; that it believeth itself judge of us all; and in addition, the news of the New World apparently reacheth His Royal Excellency even before the galleons it traveleth in. It is for this reason, my dear Balboa, that I find it necessary to dispense with thy services. Effective this moment, thou art dismissed from these offices of government and justice. May the peace of the Lord our God forever go with thee.

Happily Ever Afterly

WITHOUT BEATING AROUND the bush—after all, why waste words—let it be known: Balboa was summarily fired from his job.

The sumptuous office of the Marquis turns against him. From the wall, the portrait of King Carlos regards him accusingly, and the national flag contemplates him as though deceived. The diplomas that certify the chief as a "bona fide conquistador" shake their heads from side to side in frank disillusionment.

Conquistador Balboa remains silent until his ex-boss ends his monologue.

"Dost thou not think it well written?" asks the Marquis.

"Impeccable."

"And the contents?"

"Absorbing."

"Any comments?"

"Judging from the clouds, it looks like rain to me."

"And what else?"

"It's going to rain."

"What else?"

"The fields will be wet, and green will be our favorite color."

"And?"

"White and red. Above all red."

"I don't understand."

"The passing of years shall give us independence, two empires, reform, the Porfirian dictatorship and the Revolution."

"What art thou trying to say?"

"The people will rise up triumphant."

"Yes, yes. May the peace of the Lord our God forever go with thee."

Balboa the Conquistador, on the way to his house, an uncertain future, head bowed, ponders the current situation, considering:

**This is not the best way
to begin a marriage that was supposed to be lived
happily ever afterly.**

The Happiness You Seek and Keep on Seeking

WALKING DOWN THE STREET on the way to his house, Balboa thinks a series of thoughts that he's never entertained before. In ideas and words that normally would never occur to him, his mind is visited by the hackneyed matter of man's existence on earth.

Seeking happiness: that's what it's all about. The eternal quest. The obstacles and stumbling blocks that come and go in life.

As he walks down the street, recently laid off and without a doubloon to his name, his head lights up with scenes from the distant 20th century.

The street on the way to his house is flooded with a thousand automobiles (a strange word, that: auto-mobile). Inside them, people are muttering because the traffic won't go forward: vile bottleneck. Cars crawl to a stop like a tired worm: because there are so many of them and the traffic signals (traffic signals?) don't do enough with their enchanted on-and-off lights. The street overflows with pedestrians (a really strange word) traveling in a rush, practically running, hurrying, faster, faster, in a dither, a lather, life won't wait, fast first faust faust.

19

Deep breathing. Constant rushing. The girls in miniskirts tend to wear scowls, their lovely faces now turned coarse. It matters not to them if a man has honorable intentions in his fingers—the miniskirt girls walk by and by and won't give you the time of day; they'll go by without stopping, every one of them an overpopulation statistic, every one a city bus (bus?), packed to the gills. The passengers squeeze up against each other with perspiring, sudoriferous, sweato-masochistic intensity. The bus joins up with the current, a worm asleep awhile ago, now backing up, hanging over, diving in, into the drink again. The wind don't blow in the big city. Hey you can't blow anymore, old man. Sorry—the world's gone modern; that's part of the daily grind.

Amen.

Then the futuristic scenes stop, waiting for Balboa to solve the following enigma: people will still be seeking happiness even in the 20th century. In this very same big city, in this same wide world.

Walking down the street, thinking about Florinda and about potential happiness that people seek and keep on seeking forever and ever (Amen to that and other things seekable but not findable), Balboa stumbles upon the none-too-pleasant reality of a bus terminal (??). It's pointing north,

The days pass by in a search for work (a gig, a job, a hustle). Eying the newspapers. The classified ads. Going house to house. Getting in long lines at the union halls to see if anyone needs another body to lend a hand for just a little bit, a little while at least. The whole thing makes me uncomfortable, because if I had a normal job I wouldn't be telling this story.

like a just-fired crossbow, for the simple reason that in the year fifteen hundred something-or-other, there was no work, due to lack of progress. And in nineteen hundred something—almost the year 2000—there's no work because there's too *much* progress. The conclusion in both cases is the same: leave your home, your family, your belongings, everything you have, everything essential, and travel to The Border, where New Spain ends and where begins

The Northernish Empire

Walking down the street to his house, the 20th century show finished playing in his head, Balboa practices the words he will use on Florinda to convince her of the inevitability of his expedition to the North. Sweet words, comforting words, whose meanings leave no doubt about the possibility of happiness and about his quest through time.

And she, Florinda, his love, will go with him. Not because his arguments are so convincing (he's never been much of an orator), but because of this thing about a quest—such a noble word.

Her man seeks the happiness that she has found since the very moment she chose to love him forever.

And that's the truth.

Florinda Speaks

ROSARIO TOLD ME…
No.

I'd better not call her Rosario Rosario. She doesn't like it. Better say Auachtli Auachtli because that's what she likes to be called. OK. I'll start over:

Auachtli told me…

No.

Her name is Rosario. The padre told me it's better to say Rosario because if I don't the padre scolds me, the padre hits me, he hits me. Rosario is her name. Even though she doesn't like it. That's her name and that's that.

I'll start over.

My best friend. That's it.

My best friend tells me—because no matter what her name is, no matter how old she is, no matter how fat, she's my best friend—that I should never think twice when I get an idea, that I should just carry it out immediately and act, act as soon as something comes into my head, as soon as it's in my thoughts. I should do it. And if not? If not, life takes away your ideas, it takes them away. She always tells me I was born on a good day and because of that, nothing I do, nothing I decide will come out bad.

My friend laughs with her strong, loud laugh; not a low laugh, her laugh. Laughter, laughing. She's always laughing, always showing me a good time. Her name is Auachtli and it's good to call her that because it's her name and it's her mother's name and her grandmother's name. Don't let anyone call her any other name. Not even the padre. Don't let anyone ever say anything except what my friend wants to hear.

Here we go again.

Auachtli—my sister my grandmother my friend my bosom buddy—tells me I was born on a good day, Day One of the Deer is my day, and she, too, was born on this same day and she's a good person, and I'm a good person. She has told me so, Auachtli has, she was there to catch me. My little head fell into her hand and she said Good Morning to me and even though I didn't know how to say anything, I didn't know how to talk, I mean I'd just come into the world, I said Good Morning to her too. And Auachtli smiles when she hears me now, she calls me silly girl but she says it with affection, with a sweet voice, with soft words, her laughter, laughter as strong as the laughing laughter of the sky, thelaughter of rainstorms, of thunder, of lightning. Her laugh.

I want to tell her but I can't—I want to talk to her about him but I mustn't. She wants the best for me, she's always said that; but she wants me at her side, she's not letting me go. I'm her only one, her only one, she shouts this to me, she whispers it. I'm the one who comes and helps her when she's sick. I'm the one who makes her *atole*, who rubs her arms and legs. There's no one else in her life, she shouts this to me, she whispers it. But I have to do what I have to do and if my man needs me, what can I do, Auachtli, what can I do with his eyes resting upon me

23

except go with him wherever he's going, with his Uncle Decoroso and Aunt Onelia, to the Northernish Empire where life is better? That's why I'm here: not to tell you my secret but so you'll talk to me about the future, so you'll throw your corn kernels to the ground and tell me that everything will be all right, that thanks to Day One of the Deer, *everything* will be all right.

Except right now she's got *pulque* on her breath. My friend isn't walking straight. She says it's from old age old age but I know it's from *pulque* from *pulque*. It doesn't matter. I like her this way. It doesn't matter that Mom and Dad don't like her. And it doesn't matter that the padre doesn't like her. She's my friend and I like to be with her, leaning on her belly so she can comb my hair, slowly, slowly. So she can tell me she used to be a lot like me, looked so much alike; she was thin, with a little nose, and her wide mouth and eyes.

My friend gets serious, she's almost crying she's so serious. Crying, crying. All those memories and the past come into her head so strong, like pain, like the wind blowing down trees. They come to her and there's no way to comfort my friend.

"Little Flower," she says to me, "where are my children and my family? Where have they gone?"

She talks to me in that language of hers, the language from olden times, that language of mine. I understand her because I still remember it. My dad doesn't want me to remember but yes I do, I really do remember.

"Little Flower," she says, "you stay pretty; don't be like me, don't get as big as a tree, don't get all fat like this, don't let your legs swell nor your stomach grow; don't do it, Little Flower. Let your heart grow but nothing else."

There's no way to comfort my friend. She gets sad, I get sad. She won't throw her grains of corn to the ground, she won't wish me good luck. The *pulque* won't leave her in peace. It leaves her sick, like she's no good, like a lifeless stone. My sad, sad friend. And me sad, sad too. Goodbye Auachtli. I'm going home: it's for the best.

She's Leaving Home

WEDNESDAY MORNING at five o'clock as the day begins.

Mom is awake, making the corn meal dough, making tortillas. Dad asleep. Florinda very quietly waiting for her mom to leave like she always does, to buy her things, her fruit and vegetables. Florinda waits.

She leaves the message that she thought would say more. As she goes through the kitchen barefoot, her bandaged foot feels the cool floor, the cold ground. It occurs to her that she may never feel it again. The fire either. Or the smell of kindling wood or its heat. The big old household rooster. The hens or the turkey. The rooster won't crow in her new world. It won't even be the same sun coming through the same window to touch her eyes. Not the same anything. Not anymore.

Florinda puts on her new sandals that she almost never wears but which Balboa likes so much. Conquistador Balboa: are there not traces of magic in his name? Does it not shine; does his image not gleam in one's head like damp earth?

Dad is snoring, sleeping. His anger will be the worst, no way around that. He's never laughed. He never talks. He just gets mad. That's what he does best. Anger and more anger in the morning because breakfast isn't ready. Anger and more anger at work-hard-work. Anger and more anger at home, at night, because the food is the same, because everything is the same. Mom yells. Dad yells. They've changed like the weather but the weather goes back to being the same and they won't go back, they're lost. Everyone, each one, in their own world. Here at home: two worlds.

Florinda's leaving home after living alone for so many years.

Friday morning at nine o'clock and she's far away.

Goodbye goodbye.

The Message She Thought Would Say More

To MY PARENTS:

I wish this would say more and that it was clearer, or—I don't know—that you could understand it. You'll probably say I was always like a hare, hopping from field to field and never finding a home. I am that. And more.

If my leaving does any good at all, maybe it will bring you two together, bring you back home, make the two of you one home again.

Dear parents:

Another world awaits me. I think it's a better one. I don't know. But it can't be any worse.

Traveling by Three Stars

BALBOA AND FLORINDA, bound for The Border of New Spain on a Three Stars bus—seat numbers 25 and 26—holding hands, wide-eyed. The bus travels the highway while forests, deserts, towns and cities pass by the window.

Reality moves at 55 mph.

"I think my stomach hurts," he says, and she looks at him without knowing what to do. Really worried. She could recommend a bit of tea with medicinal herbs that would give him relief, but the bus most likely is not equipped with such amenities. And the bus driver is a big grouch, sitting up front, hands on the wheel, day and night, flipping flipping the same cassette cassette, oblivious to the world.

No point asking him.

"What can I do for you?" she asks him, and he understands how good it is to have her by his side. He feels relieved just knowing she's there. Soap opera love.

I will love thee with persistence, although thou be the cause of my digestive affliction, dearest Florinda, milady, because thou art forever eating, always eating and it does no good when I try to turn down thy invitations to partake—your sweet and smiling face, offering me Fritos with chili, potato chips, sodas, Hostess Twinkies.

Balboa concentrates, and it's better like this. He closes his eyes and squeezes Florinda's hand.

Furnished House

THE BIG GROUCH comes up and shakes Balboa. The day comes into his eyes like into a newly occupied house. He opens the doors to his unconscious and Balboa discovers that the walls have just been painted. Through the windows the big grouch appears, shouting: "We're here, we're here already so get off, it's about time. Whaddaya think, that this is some hotel and I'm the manager and that this is a boarding house and I charge by the room and I'm a nice guy and my wife cooks fancy meals for you that come with the rent?"

The big grouch shakes him again, mutters, talks through his teeth and leaves the bus in search of new cassettes. They've arrived. They're on The Border, at the bus station. New Spain of the Deep Blue Sea reaches all the way down here, and it's looking good, real good. The bus is already empty.

Balboa touches Florinda's shoulder and the day comes into her eyes like into a newly occupied house. In the bedroom of this house, atop a table, there's a color TV. The girl has never seen a color TV, not to mention a black-and-white one, much less a videocassette player.

They both yawn.

She gets the bag of clothes and he takes down the two boxes

30

where they carry their everything. They climb off the bus and step into The Border.

They look at each other (The Border at Florinda, Florinda at Balboa, Balboa at The Border and at Florinda), but say nothing because it's been proven, scientifically proven, that the voice is the last thing to return when one has just woke up.

He unties one of the boxes, takes out his two-cornered helmet, and crowns his head with it. He turns to Florinda, seeking her approval. She gives it without reservation and smiles broadly. "Stupendous" would be a good word to say, but she merely looks at him in a certain way and with a certain gesture, so that he can do no more than lift Florinda's hand (her noble, dark-skinned hand with its five fingers, five fingernails and its slight scar on the back) and kiss it in that 16th-century way he does things.

Florinda smiles with her elegant lips and utters her first pure-Border phrase:

"Man, I'm hungry."

Which goes to show that they're awake and that the new house of their unconscious is furnished and ready to live in, TV and all.

Adiós, Conquistador, Adiós

VICTIM OF A SHIPWRECK in the cold waters of The Border, Balboa swims, fighting for survival. He sees the remains of the ship sinking forever into the furious deep blue sea that rises and falls, falls and rises. Balboa is condemned to perish. Balboa is condemned to sink just like his comrades on the voyage. Loneliness enters through his left leg, pulling on him, abusing him. The storm won't end; it pushes, presses into him, carries him off. Damned solitude: look what the deep blue sea has done with the poor conquistador. What will become of him and his adventures? When will he be able to write his chronicles, his true story? Goodbye, Conquistador, goodbye. Lovers and friends will weep. Of that there's no doubt. You shall be wept over by children you never had, by women you were still to meet. Your future holds no hostile in-laws. You will never be a world-boxing champion nor an expert oboist— assuming you ever wanted to be—because your life is passing before your very eyes, sinking. It doesn't know how to swim or float: it was never a Boy Scout, there was never anyone around to teach it even the simplest things about water. The pitiable life of the conquistador. Nobody to save him. The deep blue sea has won this battle. It's The Sad Night, La Noche Triste, the night of

Cortez's defeat. But what can you do? It's defeat, no prisoners taken. Your body, Balboa, gets more tired with each useless stroke, with each jerking kick. A cramp hits your left leg. Let it pass. Accept defeat. Let the salt water take you down. Stop fighting. Write THE END to this chapter. Say goodbye to the clouds, the sky. Say goodbye to the teller-girls at the multinational banks whom you like to look at so much and who let you look at them. All is lost, and the furious deep blue sea that rises and falls, falls and rises, doesn't forgive and doesn't forget. Soon you'll have it in your mouth and nose. Soon darkness will surround your body and you'll be dragged to the bottom, amid rocks and exotic fish that shine with their own bottom-feeding light. Goodbye, Conquistador, goodbye. You're gone forever—goodbye.

The deep blue sea burps.

Victim of a shipwreck at the bus station on The Border of New Spain, Balboa lifts his eyes and the storm clears: Florinda comes back from the bathroom.

Where To?

THE BORDER WAKES UP, stretches, takes a shower and opens its portals to admit the waves of people who pour through in buses and cars and cabs; all of them traveling, all crossing each other's paths and interconnecting, all commuting enormous distances because the day is starting and it will not wait. No matter how early you get up, no matter whether you set your alarm for the right time or earlier, the hours will catch up with you, bemused, smiling, mocking.

Where to?

Looking at his piece of paper, Balboa reads aloud, with his Spaniard's lisp, the street name and address. The first Norteño he runs into answers with that tone that's so polite it sometimes gets irritating: "Certainly. Take this bus, get off at the corner grocery store, walk three blocks, turn right, and just across from the auto shop you'll find what you're looking for."

Balboa doesn't find these directions very "There you'll find a green house," the Norteño goes on, "with white frame windows, a garden of geraniums and roses, and a sign on the fence warning of a dog no one has ever seen. You will also find a tree that smells at night, that waits for darkness to release its perfume. Many times I have seen the house you're looking for," the Norteño continues. "I have walked in front of it, I have stopped to

34

difficult and he appreci-
ates the help. Florinda
smiles admiringly at her
man. He knows every-
thing, grasps everything.
He's really on top of things.

Balboa and Florinda

look at it. I remember a woman I used to
love. I remember the touch of her small
hands (you should have seen them: so tiny
next to mine, 'nobody, not even the
rain…'), her carnival smile, her dark eyes
that stared at me from her fair face, all of
which I had to say goodbye to. It was
necessary. I had to say goodbye.

aboard the city bus, wide-eyed and all ears. The Border of New
Spain spreads out, revealing contents of streets and people who
wait. The Border is a long wait. Evidence for this: the lines of
cars at the international bridge, the all-nite liquor stores.

The Border is a long anticipation, but at the same time it's
a longer desperation, one that comes when it's not invited—
usually at lunch time.

Hands on a Clock

AT TIMES Balboa and Florinda are like the hands on a clock. Always together, with the same destination, but so unlike each other that you can't help wondering, How can these two possibly be a couple?

Balboa the second hand, totally hasty, impatient, spinning around the clock face. Meanwhile, Florinda the minute hand, barely advancing a step before stopping to contemplate the next one.

Like hands on a clock.

Balboa can't stop squirming in his seat while he waits to spot the grocery store that will mean they've gotten where they're going. He curses every time the bus stops to let off a passenger or pick one up. He crosses his arms, scratches his nose and tugs at his beard.

Florinda, sitting ramrod straight like her mother taught her, looks at the people and the cars that the bus goes past. She thinks how they're like memories; how they get passed up and forgotten after awhile, then left in your recollections like life's other events—there's no other way they can be. She feels Balboa's damp hand in constant motion, clasping and unclasping hers. She smells the scent of the other passengers' sweat lotion cologne food cigarettes grime soap, and she enjoys the atmosphere. She hears her lover's "goddamns" and "oh shits" blending with the traffic and with the city's whistles, murmurs and vendors' cries. All this goes into her mind like memories collected in a photo album, ready to be taken and looked through any time. And though it would be hard to show them to other people the way you do snap shots, you could definitely talk about them with dignity: about her memory of the first bus, the first mailman, the first flower vendor, the first people on The Border who accidentally brushed against her when they passed her on the street. It's The Border. It's the city bus. It's Balboa, tugging his beard and biting his nails like a child on his first trip to an amusement park.

Fabada

DECOROUS AND ONELIA talk about their nephew Balboa with profuse enthusiasm. The colors of Old Spain are etched in their faces. Memories surface like things that never should have sunk. Balboa was a beautiful child, fair-skinned, cute, very naughty but well-meaning.

"Aunt, please," the conquistador interrupts, with an obvious blush on his bearded cheeks.

Onelia looks through the drawers, under folded clothes that smell of moth balls. She finds photos of the baby conquistador in his birthday suit, lying on his stomach in bed, his little head raised, smiling, fat-cheeked and chubby, with a cheerful picture of the Sacred Heart of Jesus in the background.

"Please, Aunt!"

...doesn't...

Decorous insists that his nephew stand up so they can measure how wide his shoulders are and how tall he is. What a kid! Before, he was skinny, a runt, nothing like what you are now, a grown man, for godsake.

...my sweet...

But tell us, how long have you been gone? Remember, don't forget to write home; they need to know where you are. It's fine to be a conquistador but you've got to be responsible too.

…beloved Florinda…

So what are your plans? What brings you all the way up here? Things aren't so good here as people think—it's full of Indians here, bad elements from the South. The Border's just not what it used to be.

…have beautiful…

Onelia decides it's time for lunch.

Decorous knows just what his nephew needs. He understands what men want so he says get ready, winks at him, tells him to take a shower and put on some cologne because they're going out.

Onelia smiles. She sees that her nephew really has changed. So elegant! Such a man! She realizes that he's with a girl who's as dark as cooked beans. She mentions this to her husband and Decorous checks Florinda out for a few minutes.

…black eyes…

"What did you say your name was?" he asks, after considering several other questions not worthy of mention.

"Florinda."

…like no one else…

"So what exactly do you do?"

"Do?"

"How old did you say you were?"

…like no other thing…

"They say I just turned seventeen. But they say I look a lot older, too."

Decorous furrows his brow, his mouth, and everything else.

…like nothing…

Reluctantly, Onelia teaches Florinda the secrets of cooking fabada.

…like everything…

Fabada

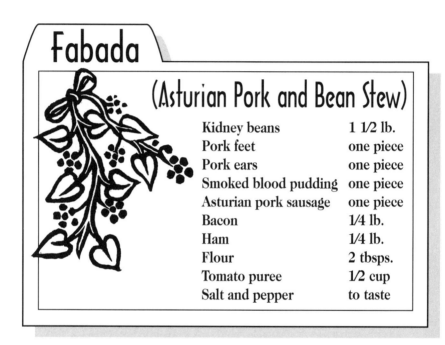

(Asturian Pork and Bean Stew)

Kidney beans	1 1/2 lb.
Pork feet	one piece
Pork ears	one piece
Smoked blood pudding	one piece
Asturian pork sausage	one piece
Bacon	1/4 lb.
Ham	1/4 lb.
Flour	2 tbsps.
Tomato puree	1/2 cup
Salt and pepper	to taste

In a Presto pressure cooker, fry the flour in a little oil. When the flour starts to brown, add tomato puree until completely mixed.

The meat should be diced and fried before-hand, starting with the pork foot and ear.

When they begin to brown, continue with the ham, the Asturian pork sausage, and finally the bacon crumbled in small pieces.

In the Presto pressure cooker with the tomato mixture, add the kidney beans, which have been soaking since the night before. Then add the blood pudding and the fried meat with enough water to fill the bowl three quarters full. Season to taste with salt and pepper and cover tightly.

NOTE: If the kidney beans are large, the stew will take about two hours to cook, but if small, only one hour. If the stew turns out too thick, add more water. Also add the juices from the meat.

Gargantuan Gertrudis

ON TOP OF A TABLE, amid scandalous music and with the audience's attention upon her, Gargantuan Gertrudis moves her body and her miniskirt right in front of Balboa and Decorous. They gaze at her and gaze. They ogle her gargantuan legs; her flirtatious face full of makeup: red lips and blue eyelids. She leans down, she rises up and moves her hips shoulder waist bellybutton and other miscellaneous things. She takes off her clothes and leaves them lying where they may. Miniskirt and croptop flee as if they'd been prisoners of Gertrudian beauty. She shows off a bikini, one so little that it must be hard for her to put it on without assistants. It's so tiny that Decorous and his nephew can get a peek at what they're not supposed to see but which they can have for a price. The music never stops; the volume just seems to increase, even if it's all only in Balboa's head. Looking at the woman going from one side of the stage to the other, he has to turn his head a little this way and that to see the whole show. She puts one of her legs up by Balboa. Without even thinking, Decoroso caresses the soft, gargantuan calf of beautiful Gertrudis, bathed in red lights and amazement. Decorous gets as far as her knee, but Gertrudis lets him know when enough is enough. Still dancing, she holds out two fingers, the index and the thumb, and rubs them together. "Money," she declares. "You gotta pay," she insists. Actually, she only moves her lips without uttering a sound, because there's so much music that it's impossible to move without stepping on it or hitting it with your elbow. Uncle Decoroso burps an "Excuse me," and when the noise stops, he's the first to get to Gertrudis, take her on his arm, and repair to a nearby hotel.

The music starts again. Splendiferous Serafina starts her dance and her striptease.

Balboa isn't alone for long. Soon, Knockout Natividad sits by him and says "Buy me a beer?" The conquistador doesn't understand, and she pretends she's mad. She gets the urge to leave but before she does, she says it again: "*¿Me invitas una cerveza?*" "*Creo que sí,*" he answers. She asks for a whisky and a scrap of paper. Balboa still doesn't understand. Not because he's naive, but because everything has happened so fast: it hasn't been even fifteen minutes since Gertrudis, Serafina and Natividad came on— all of them so superlative and fair-skinned—and his uncle hasn't come back. A shudder betrays him, from insecurity or whatever. It'd be better to go home to Florinda, who isn't gargantuan and doesn't have big breasts and doesn't dance and shake her privates as though she'd just been blessed by the Holy Father. No, she is what's right for him, what's just and good. Natividad slides her hand under the table and touches Balboa's privates as if she were consecrated—damned woman!—by the Holy Father; as if she held the Apostolic Catholic Church in her fingers; as if God himself were manipulating them. Decoroso and Gertrudis come back separately. The uncle is smiling, very happy, super-proud of his nephew, who's got Natividad touching his ☺. The uncle's hands smell like ☺, too. There's no getting around it: Balboa is upset. Decoroso is laughing, laughing, scratching his ☺, stretching to touch Nati's ☺. Balboa is disgusted, not because he's a prude or anything (after all, he's a conquistador and conquis are widely known for their exploits), but because he is overwhelmed.

He's still thinking about Florinda, the love of his life, and it's a bitch, it's hard. Poor Florinda is surely disconcerted by his Balboesque absence, trying to sleep, tossing and turning in her bed, practically in tears, while Natividad kisses his uncle, and now her catholic hands are all over his ☺, all over everything else, too, that feels good to touch, and the uncle stammers another "Excuse me, I'm going out," but Balboa stops him and says, "Don't go, be more decorous, Uncle, please. I didn't know... I mean I thought you were different, know what I mean? Florinda. Remember her? Florinda the Beautiful is waiting for me with open arms, with her cheeks, her longing fingers. Know what I mean?

☺ ☺ ☺ ☺ ☺ ?

The uncle gives Knockout Natividad a sorry-maybe-next-time look and she doesn't much care, or at least she's not offended. Balboa is proud of himself. He has managed to resist a garden-variety seduction, succeeded in placing his love above ordinary temptation. He has succeeded in ascribing importance to that which is deserving of it. Hot damn! Succeeded! Succeeded.

"You're right," says Decoroso decorously. "The fabada's probably getting cold."

PART TWO

Why Does Love Go Away?

and though their love
was hangin' on a limb
she taught him how to dance

—NEIL YOUNG

Carta de Relación

▼

(To Lady Florinda, wife of Balboa the Conquistador, on The Border of New Spain, in the house of my Uncle Decoroso, across the street from an auto repair shop)

Northernish Empire, April 9

My Dear Lady:

Since the time when last I saw thee, life hath not been the same. Branded is my heart by thy absence, and the hours pass by and the days pass by and there is not a moment when I do not think of you milady and your companionship: of our reunion, which I long for and so much imagine.

But verily as these times and this Northernish Empire have separated us, verily shall we be reunited again in New Spain and the hour will come when I shall be able to give you a mighty embrace and laugh and cry with joy, with that which I already feel merely from thinking of thee.

Therefore, in letters and on paper, accept my kiss on thy hand, for soon shall I be by thy side to give them to you in the flesh.

Amen.

Turning 'Round the Sun

IT'S TRUE: sometimes life goes by in too much of a hurry.

Florinda, all alone since her man left, and seated at the window, was looking upon her life the way she would look at a track and field champion leaping over obstacles, trying to reach a goal that only seemed to get farther and farther away.

Florinda does the chores that Aunt Onelia tells her to. She goes back to her window and yes, it's true: sometimes life goes by in too much of...

Sometimes the movies take her mind off things, but always, inevitably, Balboa shows up on the screen: a six-foot face who is undoubtedly B, the gunman, or B, the disappointed lover, or B, fleeing from some killer. Because for Florinda, this is what this love thing is like: it's not being able to get Balboa out of her mind, not wanting to banish him from her thoughts.

What was the advice that Florinda gave one of her girlfriends a few months ago who was suffering from the same malady?

She told her, "Forget him forget him wash him right out of your hair nothing good can come of it."

And what did her friend answer?

She said, "But you don't understand, you have no idea, you

can't even imagine what it's like: it's like having a headache that doesn't ache, a sickness that's not a disease, a bitter taste that's sweet."

And what was Florinda's reaction?

She said to herself, "Tsk, tsk. Poor, poor little girlfriend of mine."

Now, Florinda, all alone since her man went away, looking out the window at the cars, at the people waiting for the bus, at the mechanics in the auto shop across the street: Tsk, tsk, poor poor Florinda.

Just barely a month ago she was walking through the barrios of her grand city Tenochtitlan, thinking of breaking out of her routine and its everyday frustrations. "A change, a change," her lungs and heart shouted. "I don't want this life, I don't like it don't like it, there's got to be something over the hills, beyond the volcanoes, past the valley, something better."

And suddenly Balboa falls from the sky like a rain different from all other rains; like a Spanish coin found in a land where mostly cocoa beans are used for trade, like peace in a world where nothing is peaceful.

There arises the first problem: what to do with the rain the coin the peace where to safekeep it what to do if it asks her for something if it gets demanding if it has needs that can't always be satisfied?

What was Florinda's impression the very first time she laid eyes on a conquistador?

She said to herself: "White, metallic, bearded—but he doesn't bathe he doesn't bathe and that's terrible terrible."

What was her friend's comment when they passed by a group of young conquis?

She said, "Aren't they divine? Aren't they like the humming-bird gods who return from war triumphant? I can almost see them fighting for me, I can almost feel them thinking of my name during dangers and bloody battles."

What did Florinda answer?

She said, "But they don't bathe they don't bathe and that's terrible terrible."

Now, Florinda, all alone—thinking of Balboa, that quality he has, that endurance, that wicked habit of not taking a bath—tells herself, "It's part of his charisma," or "It's a personal strength," or "He'd just be like everyone else if he bathed everyday." Balboa is just like the conquistadors but so different from the Mexicas, not just in his smell or his habits, but also in words, in conversation, saying "thee" and lisping his Spanish "s" as though he had something rustic in his mouth.

"Do you believe in the gods, Balboa?"

"I believe in our Lord Jesus Christ, Who is seated at the right hand of the Father."

"But do you believe that the gods got us together, Balboa?"

"I believe it was Divine Providence in Its Holy Wisdom," answered Balboa, his white face bright like a neon sign.

"But you do believe in the gods?" F insists.

"Thy gods are made of stone, my love. Has no one yet explained this to thee? What good are all those Franciscan missionaries, anyway? Shit!"

"But you do believe in the gods?"

"Oh milady," snorts Balboa.

Florinda realizes that her beloved is of another understanding, that because he comes from a different world, reality doesn't always go into his heart efficiently. There's a lot left to teach him, she thinks, and not just about gods who rise up from the fire or from butterflies.* No, he needs to be taught about life, about trees moving with the wind, about the clouds announcing rain.

Big things, Balboa, things not always visible, things impossible to touch, to limn or to imagine. The gods are made of stone but

---

* The poet predicts: "Farewell forever, then; farewell forever *butterfly.*"

50

they are much more than that. Life is what you see, Balboa, but it is much more. I do not have to be a Spaniard or a conquistador to understand that. I don't have to have crossed over volcanoes or traveled north or fought a thousand battles to know it. The world already has its colors, but you have to know how to paint life into it.

"Oh, milady," sniffs B, remembering all those self-improvement books he's read.

Later, Florinda is quiet.

Balboa is quiet.

And there is the world, also quiet, turning 'round the sun.

What Her Mom Thought

THE THING IS, Florinda wasn't like the rest of the girls in Mexicco-Tenochtitlan. Even though she didn't know that there were more things in the world (i.e., more variety in fruit people colors hats pencils makeup), she wanted more in her world. She wanted a bit of what hadn't yet been invented or discovered.

She would open her hand, look at her palm, and say, "There must be something here that doesn't exist yet." She would try to imagine it, but it was hard. Closing her eyes, gritting her teeth, perspiring somewhat, she would imagine: "It's square it's round it's green it's bitter it's heavy." But the future remained far away, and as hard as she tried, she couldn't seem to reach it. Then her mother would come in, looking at her like she had at other times, thinking, "Why can't my daughter be like the other girls?" and would try to distract her by telling her stories, trying to amuse her.

"My little one, little daughter of mine,

The future to be—who is uninvited but who comes anyhow, who arrives, who leaves when he feels like it, without telling anyone —seen here like apples from the tree in Mom's orchard. Unreachable in childhood. Accessible and sensual with Ismaelita, my grade school love; hardly of interest later, when the future to be has come and is future no more.

what will become of you? Tell me, Xóchitl, what is it that you catch on a black mountain and kill on a white mat?"

"Oh Momma, I know, I know."

"It's lice, Little Flower; you catch them on your head and kill them on your fingernail."

"Oh Momma, I know, I know."

Florinda tried to forget the whole thing and prepare the chia juice for the meal. Her silhouette moved through the kitchen like a centipede in summer.

What Her Dad Thought

WHAT FLORINDA DISLIKED most about her father was not that he was always drunk, or that he uttered only stubborn words (this was related to a generalized change in popular attitude due to the political and economic situation that prevailed in the 16th century). What irritated her most about her father—who once had been young and yearning —was that he had lost his ambitions, misplaced them, and upon realizing this, hadn't even stopped to look for them.

F used to tell Auachtli:

"Ambition is monumental. It's heavy, enormous, but it's portable, and fits inside your pocket, inside your head. You can't lose it, you can't lose it."

Auachtli would look at her with her giant, ambitious eyes.

"You're right, Little Flower, ambition is like that."

Later, Florinda would go back and find her father drunk, badmouthing the Spaniards, calling them fuckers, saying bastards, laughing at all the crap he used to tell Father Bernardino and his scribes: "We used to be like this, we were like that—talking about honor and other out-of-date things."

"No, Padre, I advise my daughter to be a good and obedient woman, an honorable virgin, not to gossip or go from house to house like a wayward mouse. Above all, I tell her not to trust men because they're usually, though not always, a bunch of good-for-nothing, no-account wretches."

Actually, Dad only spoke to Florinda to ask her for food. Every afternoon he would fling himself onto his straw mat, and in dreams of his youth, revisit the dashed hopes he'd had for young Tonaltlanezi, a daughter of aristocrats, never meant for him.

She, of noble birth, and I a humble prole.
Yet our blood is no different and our hearts are the same.

Florinda's father had absolutely no ambition, only dreams that he forgot when he woke up.

"I'm worried about Florinda," Mom used to tell him.

"It's the Spaniards," Dad would say.

"The girl has weird ideas."

"It's the Spaniards. The conquistadors. Race-mixing. Taxes. Inflation."

And, more and more, seeing Spaniards in Mexicco-Tenochtitlan was like seeing the mineral-water springs of Chapultepec and the vendors in Tlatelolco. They were unavoidable, like gunk under your fingernails or old love affairs or myopia. There were Spaniards on every corner. In Azcapotzalco, Tacubaya, Coyoacán, in the Pino Suárez subway station at rush hour. Spaniards and more Spaniards.

If He Had a Normal Job

IF BALBOA had a normal job—eight hours a day, slave-driving bosses, wisecracking co-workers, overtime, income taxes—he would come home to find Florinda lying in bed reading the crime pages of the newspaper or doing crossword puzzles.

Since Onelia and Decoroso had lent Florinda a room set apart from the house, she tried to stay in it most of the day. She would pay her daily dues (washing dishes, sweeping the floor, cooking meals, ugh ugh ugh) then go back to her room.

Onelia's life was similar to Florinda's (only she had more experience since for the past 25 years Decoroso had been leaving for some unknown job), so she distracted herself by giving her niece-in-law lessons.

LESSON ONE

Thou must push the mop hard, scrub the floor to clean it well, use hot water so the grease falls off the pans. The soap can't do it all; thou must not trust what they say in commercials...

If Balboa had a normal job, he would come home tired and in a mood to eat, but not to talk. Florinda reading a newspaper, those goddamned crossword puzzles. She would impose certain demands on her husband, using verticals and horizontals, little black and white squares.

"I understand, milady, I understand," Balboa would say in the midst of a colossal yawn.

And almost immediately a dream would begin that had nothing to do with real life. Balboa's dreams abounded with white beaches and coconut palms. With postcard-perfect sunsets and Brazilian women in tiny swimsuits.

LESSON TWO

Thou must know how to speak well and use the right punctuation (careful with commas [, , , ,] girl). Thou must not repeat thy words so much. Thou should remember the encyclical of the illustrious Horacio Quiroga: "If you want to describe this scene exactly: *a cold wind blew off the river*, human language requires these words and no more to perfectly express it."

But Balboa does not have a normal job: no eight hours or taxes or jiving co-workers. No one's heard from him since he left The Border to go into the Northernish Empire.

Time goes by and Balboa—zilch.

In his city, he belongs now to the neighborhood of the absent, the subdivision of nostalgia, the township of yesterdays and migrant memories.

LESSON THREE

Study this, girl: there's more to the world than *atole*,

57

amaranth and chia juice. The only way to a man's heart is through his stomach.

The screeching radio wakes Florinda with news of the city. A very old man makes a few remarks and takes calls from his loyal audience, who are always complaining about the authorities because they don't collect the garbage off the streets. There's no water, no water Mr. Talk Show Host. It's the governor, it's the mayor, it's life, Mr. Talk Show Host. It's politics it's corruption it's the president, Mr. Talk Show Host. A cold wind blows off the river, Mr. Talk Show Host. It will not blow again.

The city is difficult without you, My Love; its streets lose their pavement and turn back to dirt roads. The wind raises a light dust in my room and fills the empty space you've left. The buses go forward at their slow pace, and no one dares to board them.

Should She Look for Work?

Oh, WHAT TO DO? What to do? What to do?

As she stands behind four girls, the maquiladora opens its arms and welcomes her.

It's the first time she's looked for a job, and Florinda feels insecure. With a trembling hand, she writes her name, her educational background and her references on a piece of paper. She takes a test that she considers very easy: "Put an x on the round figure (§ ¶ O)." A urine sample to determine if she's pregnant. Negative of course. One of the girls: positive. *So sorry, dollface.*

Sermon delivered by the Personnel Manager:

"Welcome to the Stanton Pacific de México family.
Today all you lucky girls have been selected for
one of the best jobs in the world."

Said in English, so nobody understands.

Florinda seated on a high stool, in front of a conveyer belt that moves electronic devices.

"This is the art of soldering," a co-worker teaches her with a soldering iron.

"This is the art of timing," a supervisor shows her with a stop-watch in her hand. Thirty per minute minimum. More? Of course.

Florinda picks up the soldering iron. She burns her fingers a couple of times while her co-workers kibitz around her.

"Who's that?" asks La China.

"One of those damned Mexico City types: a chilanga," says Big City Girl.

Florinda looks at the electronic circuit boards going by on the conveyer belt. This is science. This is what has not yet been discovered. Mass production. How distant you are, my Tenochtitlan. How distant the moisture of your mornings, the scent of corn, the comings and goings of your people.

Soldering iron melt solder, solder solder circuits.

Again.

Soldering iron melt solder, solder solder circuits.

Again.

Thirty per minute. Maybe more.

Televisions

WHEN LA TELEVISIÓN opens her eye, she shows Florinda all kinds of things that Florinda supposes are part of that wisdom of the world which Auachtli mentioned to her in the good old days: i.e., those things you should strive for if you want to be a talented VIP.

Florinda gets sad when La Televisión tells love stories that disappear into time and space. She can't explain why, but she sobs over the poor Toms, Dicks and Harriets that La Televisión shows her. On the other hand, she gets happy when La Telly tells stories of people tripping as they try to carry a refrigerator up a five-story flight of stairs.

When La Televisión closes her eye, Florinda tells her own stories so that La Telly will sleep well and the evil spirits won't get into her dreams. Always they are stories with endings full of happiness and hope: dead lovers reuniting in heaven, bad people repenting, ever-faithful animals.

This is the world Florinda tells La Sweet Telly about, and it works out well: evil spirits never enter her. They stay outside or go into El Radio, very early in the morning, making him screech or play music and commercials with no warning. Damned radio.

What the Girls Think

EIGHT HUNDRED GIRLS look at her. She's the new girl. They look at her when she walks moves asks for permission looks for the restroom for fifteen minutes doesn't ask how to get there. She's one of those fucking chilangas. They look at her coming back after she's called down by Supervisor Nero. They look at her struggling with Engineer Big Lips, who's always longing to get next to her and the others as if they were spring blossoms ready for plucking. They look at her during the break, eating alone, smiling at some of the girls, trying to make friends, eating alone and coming back to solder. They look at her when she listens to the bell, when she punches her time card and leaves under the guard's scrutinizing eyes, then stands on the corner waiting for the bus. They look at her as she goes off.

Big City Girl says: She's a chilanga.

Barbie Doll says: Yeah, but what's her story?

Sufferella says: Poor girl poor girl.

La China says: It's her own business, fucking Sufferella.

In the world of La China: Everyone's on their own.

In the world of Sufferella: Nobody's perfect.

In the world of Barbie Doll: Flowers beauty love.

In the world of Big City Girl: Chilangos *Go Home.*

Radios

FLORINDA HAS PROBLEMS with one radio in particular. He's located at the head of her bed, where he watches over her, pretending he doesn't know what's going on, as if he were a complete saint who never woke her up in the morning like some monster of mass-communication. After all, there are times she'd rather sleep late so she'd have less time to wait, less time to be without Balboa.

El Radio squawks shamelessly, knowing full well that she wants to sleep. At first she'd thought he would be like her old rooster who used to wake her up back home, but then El Radio started bothering her, and often appeared in her nightmares, perched at the head of her bed while she was being chased by some demon.

Sometimes Florinda wakes up exhausted by this devil's chase and by El Radio's screeching that sounds like cackling. When that happens, she jumps out of bed and runs to La Sweet TV, hugs her and asks her for advice. La Telly opens her eye and shows a person sleeping. Florinda understands.

Once, La Telly opened her eye and a laundry detergent appeared. Florinda didn't know what she was trying to tell her, so she assumed La Telly was still dreaming and talking in her sleep.

If El Radio doesn't stop bothering her, Florinda is considering throwing him out the window. He'll see, stinking Radio; a bus will run over him and adiós he'll be gone with the gods.

Pizzas Enter Her Life Like a Pie Thrown Into Her Heart

NATURALLY it had to be Barbie Doll (who else?) who was the first to come up and talk to her. F had to smile timidly, had to tell her story, about her love for Balboa, his failure to return, her lack of money, her need for work. It's for the best, don't you think?

"Right on," says Barbie Doll. "Men are gorgeous marvelous."

It had to be Sufferella (who else?) who was the second to come up and talk to her. F had to smile while she told Sufferella about her life story, her city, her home, where the music's playing, home, where my love lies waiting, silently for me. It's for the best, don't you think?

"I hear you," says Sufferella. "You poor kid."

La China and Big City Girl don't come up. The former comments: "She's a dame like the rest of us. She's got her troubles we've got ours. We're victims of a capitalist system dominated by men."

"She's a chilanga," says the latter.

The girls hold a powwow where they discuss they amend they paraphrase. And the final vote is: three in favor, one against.

Tough luck, Big City Girl.

At the restaurant, Florinda looks for the first time upon that enormous flour tortilla with tomato sauce and melted cheese that they call pizza. The girls invite her to eat with them. She doesn't realize that with every bite of this marvelous Italian invention, her slim young figure starts to disappear.

Good Manners

FLORINDA AND BALBOA at the New Oriental Cafe. She very serious, picking her fork through the broccoli, jicama and other indecipherable vegetables. He also very serious, digging into the Cantonese chicken, which works its magic, delighting his stomach.

"Well, I'm back," the conquistador says.

Florinda nods as she looks at the white rice and soy sauce. Her fork moves of its own free will.

She'd like to tell him, "I've spent more time without you than with you. I'm no good at this, at waiting."

"I don't like The Border," she says instead. "I don't like it."

"But there's so much stuff here. Have you seen everything?"

Florinda shrugs. Balboa recalls the women who fall in love with conquistadors before they leave on their expeditions, and wait and wait for them until they return or they learn of their loved one's death.

His beloved is not like those women. His beloved is better.

When he got to his aunt and uncle's house, Florinda had looked at him through the window and hadn't wanted to open up for him: he wasn't her conquistador. She went back to washing and hanging the laundry.

"Go away," she told him from the back yard, knowing he wouldn't hear her words. "Go away."

Balboa kept knocking.

Onelia opened the door, all happy, and told Florinda: "Look who's here! Didst not thou hear him calling?"

With his armor packed up in a box, Balboa didn't seem so tall as when she first met him. He was wearing jeans and a cotton t-shirt. He wasn't her man, not with his hair short and his beard shaved off. This was not her man.

"Dost thou like it?" Balboa asks, referring to the food.

"No," she answers, referring to his appearance. "No."

Florinda has never read the *Bon Ton Dictionary of Good Manners* (by Lina Sotis, Grijalbo Publishers). Otherwise, she would have known that beards accentuate the most horrendous features in men. It's common knowledge that no woman likes bearded guys.

She wants her conquistador just as she first discovered him, without amendments or corrections.

Despite the brief time that it took her to fall in love, she's put so much effort into it that it's not easy to stop. Perhaps she feels that love sometimes goes, goes far away and then returns, as though the heart were a hotel and love an aging John, a regular with the whores. Yet she maintains a faithfulness that must be underscored: <u>faithfulness</u>.

Balboa tries to say, "I am a conquistador on the inside, not the outside. Appearances can be deceiving."

But this little saying gets lost in a sip of tea. That's the problem with eating and thinking, eating and wanting to say something, eating and wanting to be sure of love. How can he reiterate to Florinda that for him she is the New World when his mouth is full of vegetables?

Balboa thinks: "If women were things you bought, you'd know how to take care of them and would always be sure of finding them in their place."

Florinda thinks: "If men were things you bought, you'd know how to take care of them and would always be sure of finding them in their place."

But things and men.
Are different.

But things and women.
Are different.

They came to this conclusion, yet they did not speak, because of the *Manual of Urbanity and Good Manners* (by M.A. Carreño, Patria Publishers), which they had read, and which points out that one should not eat and talk at the same time.

Try and Catch the Wind

ONCE MORE they look at each other, once more their hearts beat anew and their touch is like the first touch. Tranquility. Tranquillity. Where are you? Have you ever been to the sea? In your eyes I see a brown color that sometimes turns green. Can you believe it? The color of your eyes sometimes changes in my imagination, which distorts everything. Sometimes they're green. Did you know that? Then you smile. Then your face smiles and what can I do, True Love, with your eyes resting upon me? Mornings evenings nights. Imagine. Turn on the light. Consider reincarnation—that taxi's always available—think about the possibility of other lives other times by my side by your side. Lovers? Sister and brother? Are our lives perhaps linked from a dark and distant beginning? All over again today? Yes? Living an opportune warmth that comes at the precise moment and does not go, does not leave, but remains. I blush. Really? I get intimidated. I don't think so. I share. Yes. I share the air you breathe and my voice blathering and blathering, saying silly things, things that surely are corny, profound, abstract, surrealistic, never said or understood again; thus they lose themselves, lose themselves in time and reason. What can I do, True Love, with your eyes resting upon me? Close my eyes my mouth let me gaze like an old statue in some museum we'll never visit. Are you going away? Is it time? I'd like to know what you're thinking. Is your mind a distant object? Why the doubts why the fear? Tell me: straitjacket lonely rest stop. Why no why yes. I'm talking to you, my favorite reading my simple song my sweet adjective. Explain to me why.

How Many Hands?

HE'S BACK. He's home. Once more: his trousers hanging on the chair. You look at his naked back next to you on the bed. Do you know how many of your hands it takes, one after the other, to travel up his back? Yes, of course. He is the antique vessel that you carried water with to wash your feet. Of course. It seems that his scent has changed, but it's only your sense of smell. It seems his eyes no longer look with the same intensity, but it's your eyes, myopic, that mis-judge his love. His hands seem different, but that is due to the rebellion in your body. He is a canvas recounting histories: his own codex, his chronicles. Of course. Will you sleep tonight, or will you stand vigil, looking at him?

It seems like his voice when he says the same words has lost   has lost.

Couldn't it be your ears that don't want to hear the same things?

She had already thought about that:

"What will I do with him when he comes back?"

"How much does he have to explain to me before I can believe in his love?"

"How could he think that nothing has changed?"

71

You don't dare wake him up. He is a stranger whom you once saw pass by. He is a border, a dividing line that comes nearer and nearer, trying to seize lands that, in reality, hardly belonged to him.

Question: Should you be happy that he's back?

If the theory is correct and he's a stranger again, this could be the first time you're seeing him and (see page 10) you should feel the same now; the same things should move you. Thus, waking him up would be an urgent task, an unequivocal necessity, a vertigo, or, that is to say: something pulling you into a mythical abyss which, sooner or later, all of us (All of Us) must fall into.

React like in the beginning?

Are you still that girl adorned with flowers and artifice who was introduced at the beginning of this novel?

Has enough time passed to say now that you're different?

How many times have we heard people say that a person isn't the same, thereby claiming a transformation has occurred as though making a change requires nothing more than proposing it?

I think we've changed a little.

(The insecurity is obvious.)

You've changed. Of course. And the way you look at things and your scent are different. He is the cartography that has allowed you to navigate to this conclusion.

When you sleep, will he be keeping watch over your sleep, looking at your back, asking the same questions, doubting whether he has changed—or is it that you are the stranger?

It doesn't matter.

If there was resentment (and I think there was), it can be fixed.

If there was neglect (and I think that, too), it can be fixed.

Will he want to?

Will marriage begin and will you bathe and get dressed together, each going to your own job, going toward the future with no hurry, the way you planned it once upon a time?

Do you know how many hands it takes to travel up his back?
Start over.
Together again.
Do you want to?
Does he want to?
We shall see what happens next.*

---

* The poet corrects himself: "Life is a trip on a parachute, and not what you'd like to think."

The Simplest Things

IT'S WELL KNOWN that the world turns the wrong way when the simplest things get complicated, when anger erupts for trivial reasons.

Balboa starts to get angry about insignificant things that never used to bother him before.

1. *Florinda has never been able to open a box of corn flakes.*

(And it's such a simple thing, sweet Florinda; as simple as brushing your teeth or waking up in the morning. One learns it as a child, without any need for teachers. One learns it just because one wants so much for one's mouth to fill up with those delicious corn flakes, with sugar, soaked in milk. You've always seemed like an intelligent girl, Florinda, yet thou canst not pay attention and open a box of corn flakes right. You insist on opening them from the bottom and tearing up the top. You dolt, haven't you noticed that when you open the box the rooster is upside down? I'm talking about the famous rooster that you see singing on the front of the box to show that it's best to eat them for breakfast. This famous rooster is supposed to be on his feet when you open a corn flakes box, not squatting, nor bent forward, much less on his head. What the hell is this? You tear up the box like you were helping it give birth, as though thou

74

wert a midwife and not a good-for-nothing Indian. How can you possibly close it afterwards? Tell me, will you? How can you keep bugs at night from eating up our groceries that have cost me so much suffering, so much of my life spent in hard and endless labor.

At times like this, I remember Ismaelita, my grade school love: the movement of her skirt, her enormous old patent-leather shoes, her skinny, knock-kneed legs that couldn't hold up her cotton socks.

And what do you have to say about the bag inside the box, the one that holds the flakes, that keeps them fresh and crunchy when you eat them. What do you have to say about that, huh? I'm always finding it torn and ruined. I find my breakfast dry and foul-tasting, rancid and intransigent, just because thou art incapable of opening a bag and a box with the delicacy they deserve. My God, Oh Virgin! What to do with thee, with thy ways? I don't know I don't know.)

2. *Florinda puts on her shoes first, then her panties and her dress.*

(It's unbelievable, sweet Florinda. It's not even that you're trying to be contrary; you're just going against all logic. Shit! The numerical order that we've inherited from past centuries, since that bastard Pythagoras. Damn. Besides, you insist on walking around the house naked with your unmentionables hanging out. You get a glass of water and turn on the stove without a stitch on you except shoes and socks. Tell me how a man could keep from feeling enraged by such barbaric habits. I don't want to lose my temper, my little Indian, but thou art drawn to stupidity the way dogs are drawn to car tires and fire hydrants. I swear many times have I seen thee struggle to put your shoes on first, then your panties, then your dress. I don't know any other woman who does it this way, and with luck, the world will see only a few more like thee.)

3. *Florinda doesn't…*

For a long time now, Florinda's and Balboa's world has been turning in the wrong direction.

What Happened Next

▼

WHEN SHE WOKE UP, the conquistador was already gone.

Why Does Love Go Away?

FLORINDA WAKES UP with Onelia's hand on her forehead. The fever has gone. It has left thy body, Florinda; I think you're better, I think you can get up and go out and take a walk, mop the floor, wash the dishes…I think you're better.

Florinda wakes up again after Onelia leaves. Yes, it's true, she no longer feels sick. She sniffles a little. She gets rid of the drip in her nose with the back of her hand; she tastes it and discovers something: it's water from a sea dripping out, a lukewarm sea, pleasant sea. Her throat doesn't hurt. There's not so much heat in her body. A bit of cold makes her cover herself, pull the blankets up to her neck.

Why does love go away? she asks herself.

Why doesn't it stop and wait?

It's very odd, this impatience of love.

At first she would have died to see Balboa.

Later she died of sadness. He'd sent barely one letter, with so few words in it that she imagined him lost in a jungle that would be impossible to rescue him from. Fruitless expeditions would be in vain, as would notifications to the authorities and investigations. Balboa had gotten lost of his own free will. Florinda thought that restless love had made a very brief stop in the heart of her man. It waited there a few minutes, but fatigue and boredom quickly forced it out in search of new lands.

This is what Florinda thinks as she lies covered up to her neck.

This is what she'd been thinking once while waiting in a long line at the tortilla shop. But back then, she blamed herself for being so selfish, for not believing in her Balboa working for the two of them, having to put up with nasty bosses, working unpaid overtime, just to come back and be by her side.

Silly Florinda silly Florinda.

Didn't you tell Balboa once that money wasn't necessary for happiness, that a poor conquistador would be sufficient, enough for you? "How dumb," you tell yourself at the market while you finger the tomatoes in order to pick out the best kilo. "How dense," you yell at yourself in the laundromat during the rinse cycle. "What a dolt," you reproach yourself while you sweep the floor and wash the dishes.

Poor little love of mine, and me so cruel.

She couldn't fix the exact moment when she felt that love had left her heart.

It was odd, love's impatience. As though upon tiring of waiting for the bus, it had decided to catch a different one on another route, to a place that was hidden and unsuspected only a few days earlier.

Sick Florinda lonely Florinda.

Absent Balboa distant Balboa.

Again.

Why does love go away? she asks as she lies covered up to her neck.

The Letter Didn't Stay
With Her Forever

FLORINDA is one of those odd people who keep everything they're given. But since most of what she'd received in her life (dolls, flowers, earrings) had been left behind, she decided the letter would be a symbol of all these things.

Thus, Balboa's letter (*Branded is my heart by thy absence...*) could also be:

a) the flower that a certain Hernán Tezozómoc once gave her during one of those mornings at church and which, after mass, she had safeguarded between two pieces of wood tied with a cord;

b) the set of drawings that said Hernán Tezozómoc did for her depicting them walking through Chapultepec, with glyphs coming from their mouths as though they were conversing; he never taking her hand, but always changing the subject, talking about his cousin—what did he say his name was?—about his job, about the things kids talk about when they're kids and don't have anything to say to each other;

79

c) the same Tezo-, gone, not there anymore nor does it matter (-zomoc) because he suddenly decided to take off with another chick, one less weird, less Florinda; and

d) the avenues and the water-filled canals that people traveled on in her distant city.

Did the letter stay with her forever?

She keeps it as though it were a piece of underwear. Florinda liberates herself from her other clothes, goes to bathe, and the paper gets wet from the hot water's steam. She sticks the letter to the bathroom wall, looking at it there while she soaps her hair and scrubs her panties. The words of Balboa (...*and the hours pass by and the days pass by and there is not a moment when I do not think of you milady*) grow longer and slide down like tears; they change their meaning, they tell her things they hadn't said before. She closes her eyes so the soap won't get in. When she opens them again, the letter is not a letter. It's a mush of paper without writing, barely hanging on the wall, as though it must hang there so as not to lose that deepest part that makes it more a letter and less a paper mush. She closes her eyes. When she opens them again the wall is bare. The paper, what's left of it, lies at her dark feet, between her toenails, turning round and round, sliding down the drain, together with the water with the soap with everything else.

Did the letter stay with her forever?

No.

The letter did not stay with her forever.

Not Sadness

NOT SADNESS. It's something else. If she drove a car it would be like a lonely ride down a coastal highway. Intense rain banging against the windshield. Night falling. The lights of other cars spreading against the glass like the yolk of an egg.

Not sadness.

Something has happened to him, something immense outsized small tiny. It's the same but it's not. He has left, leaving behind his box full of conquistador things, his conquistador world, conquistador life.

"Am I part of his things of his life of his world?" F asks herself.

Then, a phone call.

Could it be him, contrite?

"It's a woman's voice," says the aunt.

Not sadness. It's something else. If she were a man she would put her hands in her pockets and take a walk on the beach. A lonesome car would pass by the man Xóchitl, without noticing him. The night. The lights. Other men walking with their hands in their pockets.

Not sadness.

La China tells her a bit about the world:

For years I lived with a man who was unsure of his love for me. When he walked out of my life, I was filled with sadness and with great relief. Across the street from my house these days, there's a guy living who looks at me every morning when I go out. He's shy, you can tell: he hardly shows his face through the curtains but he's as punctual as the arrival of Mondays. He's there in the afternoons, too, waiting for me to come back (his brown eyes). What should I do with him, Florinda? Go to him and tell him to fuck off? Wait for him to come to me, to call me, ask me to dinner, to the movies, to fuck, then tell him to fuck off? I am a supermarket full of doubts, girlfriend: retail, wholesale, on sale, pounds of doubts. The same thing happened to me with another man, and now I'm supposed to be smart enough not to let it happen again. Don't tell anyone, girlfriend. Not even the girls. It's not my style to screw up like this.

Not sadness. It's something else. It's the air that circulates in your lungs, the telephone cord, the distant voice speaking from another part of the city.

She tells La China a bit about the world:

In my homeland everything is different, Chinita. You can't imagine, and it didn't even seem that way to me until now. There are no cars, no planes, no telephones. People greet each other in the mornings with broad smiles, with heart and with fresh red prickly pear fruits in their hands. We are surrounded by water. In Texcoco, the moon shining in Texcoco, waves of light rise up rise up when the wind comes down from the volcanoes. Nothing nothing is the same. Even so, in front of my house, a boy looks out every morning, waiting for my return. He never talked to me about waiting. I never said anything to him about love. He stares out through the curtains (his brown eyes), regretting having let me go. His constant breathing, his days going by going by.

Naturally La China doesn't understand.
Thanks anyway.
Us girls are all getting together at seven.
Nah, not this time, Florinda tells her.
Not sadness.
Just an urge to drive on the rainy coast and look for the man walking alone, hands in his pockets, paying no attention to the passing lights getting farther away, moving along like this story.

What Florinda Seeks in Life

▼

1. Happiness.

2. A dog.

3. Someone to give her a foot massage when she's tired.

4. Her own house with a garden.

5. That spark, those fireworks, that hearth to warm her feet on winter afternoons.

6. An automatic washing machine.

7. The scent of a night-blooming tree in her garden.

8. An end to abuse by the authorities.

9. No more sexual harassment from the bosses.

10. Love?

PART THREE

Life and Work in the Northernish Empire

we get so strange
across the border

—PETER GABRIEL

In Which B's Obsession for F is Spoken of and His Favorite Reading Material Described

FLORINDA MEANT far more to him than the deep blue sea that he loved so much to cross. She meant far more than the creaking of the galleons on their voyages to distant lands. Florinda was the highest good, the road to peace and quiet that every man wishes for in life. For Balboa, she was the reason for his expeditions, she was what he'd read in his books about knighthood, she was that ambition without peer for which he must defend the weak and frail in the Holy Name of the King. With her he could find within him all that can be found, according to his self-help books.

His favorite titles:
How to Win Friends and Keep Them for Two Weeks
Learn to Say "I Can"
The One-Minute Conquistador
Why Older Men Prefer Younger Women

When Balboa looked at Florinda's black eyes for the last time, before his Uncle Decoroso closed the trunk he'd be traveling in to get to the Northernish Empire, he felt that tidal wave every sailor dreads, the final defeat that all soldiers eventually come to know.

Leaving her was like lowering the flag in a signal of defeat. It was like the last shots fired from the blunderbusses, the inevitable surrender that can no longer be postponed if you want your comrades-in-arms to survive.

For him, leaving her was something that was never supposed to happen.

And Florinda's eyes, Florinda's face, Florinda's lips—his beloved —resonated a thousand ways in his head.

Wise and Not So Wise Words Uttered By His Parents During that Long-ago Childhood in Madrid

WHAT WAS IT his father had said to him once in the Madrid of his longings?

"When it comes to women, never give them all of your love, all of your money, all of your happiness or all of your time. Remember, Sunday is your day for watching soccer. Remember, weekdays are for working."

What was it that Balboa had answered?

"Oh Dad, what women are you talking about, seeing as how there's none that I love?"

His dad, a tall, bearded man who loved soccer, defined his life this way:

"Men never find happiness because it's always right in front of them."

He repeated this anytime he got the chance.

Then he'd add: "Men are always looking for something without knowing what it is."

And he repeated this anytime he got the chance.

Balboa's mother, a massive woman who used to sweep the same

place on the floor over and over again as though it were a dusty piece of her soul, corrected him:

"Don't believe that, my child. Seeking without knowing what you're looking for is a game for fools. Good men always find, and they always love.

"Don't confuse the boy, you old bag."

"Don't put stupid ideas in his head, you dumb Cossack."

Balboa decided to seek, as his father told him, but also to find and to love, like his mother recommended. He lay down to sleep thinking about all this, while his parents' screeching voices lulled him as they so often had in the past.

Random Phrases that Came into the Conquistador's Mind While Traveling in the Trunk of Uncle Decoroso's Car

In old age, one should travel on level ground, with neither ups nor downs.

Ups and downs are best during one's youth.

Money.

Not enough to be a millionaire and have yachts and Brazilian women in bathing suits. Not that much.

But definitely enough to at least live in peace, to put on a pair of slippers and watch soccer on TV while Florinda talks on the phone, reads, sleeps or whatever.

Happiness.

Is money a means for achieving happiness?

Happiness = peace + quiet + kids +
economic security.

Or is happiness just an excuse to go on an
eternal quest for riches?

Carbon monoxide.

It smells like smoke in the trunk.

Claustrophobia. Death.

How long has it been? Are we in
the Northernish Empire yet?

Did I do the right thing,
leaving my beloved alone
and going on a lark where
you have to cross over in
a car trunk?

Decisions.

The car stops.

In the Northernish Empire Where Life is Better Or If It's Not At Least It Seems Like It Is

OPENING THE TRUNK of his Uncle Decoroso's car, in which Balboa just crossed The Border of New Spain, all the marvels of the world entered and enveloped him like a Pandora's Box turned inside out. He had no doubt: he had discovered El Dorado, a feat much grander than all those performed by Cortez, Pizarro or his namesake, Nuñez de Balboa, even if all of their feats had been consolidated and judged by history.

In our conquistador's newly discovered world, luminous ads emerged from the ground like new stars. The streets were wide and clean. Lofty supermarkets rose up, brimming with food and with winsome checkout girls. People were friendly, and they said "thank you," for everything they received and "'scuse me," for every mistake they made (or at least that's how Decoroso explained it, now that he'd turned into a translator, just as Geronimo de Aguilar and Malinche once had been).

"That's an ad for cigarettes," said his uncle, and the nephew learned about tobacco for the first time.

There's a hotel," the uncle explained, and the nephew confirmed the occurrence of circumstantial love.

"That's a late-model car going down the 805 freeway," and Balboa perceived the luxury of materialism; for a second he dreamed of lines of credit and checking accounts; and he yearned for a job with gorgeous secretaries and annual vacations in the Caribbean.

"Now I understand, Uncle—this really is the New World, the one that must be conquered."

Decoroso understood. He, too, had once seen the Northernish Empire for the first time and had felt the same emotions. Accompanied by his faithful wife Onelia, he had tried to discover and conquer, to rule and glorify, until he understood: all is a mirage; nothing is as easy to attain as it seems.

The uncle smiled: "Everything is within your reach, Son, everything you could possibly want.

"Just be careful of the Border Patrol. They are dreadful beings, half-man, half-beast…" and for starters, he pointed out a Mexican restaurant:

Such was Balboa's destiny, his beginning. The start of his conquest: a pile of dirty plates.

She's Not Completely Catholic

SOMETIMES, during brief bouts of insomnia, when the woman he loved entered his thoughts as she would an auditorium full of people, Balboa thought that his feelings for Florinda could overcome any obstacle.

Was not distance perhaps the hardest test? Or perhaps the cruelest impediment was his inability to write a letter. If there really is love in this tale—and everything seems to indicate that there is—shouldn't it be enough for him to know that his beloved exists, even if she's in another part of the world, thinking about him, living for him?

Or maybe Florinda wasn't convinced that Balboa's Spaniard love was permanent. Perhaps she didn't believe that he, being far away, could handle shields, swords and love all at the same time.

Maybe fleeting memories alone were not enough to sustain her love. Maybe she needed something more tangible—much more so than a photograph or a memento. Maybe a physical presence: a back, arms, legs, ankles, etc.

Florinda with another man?

If only she were a little more Catholic, she wouldn't have so many doubts about blindly believing in the intangible. Distance wouldn't be distance, and Balboa's absence would be the fundamental thing in life with which to prove her Faith.

But she's not completely Catholic.

Florinda with another man?

A test? An obstacle?

It was just a brief bout of insomnia.

Advice from Fat Charlie, The Archangel

FAT CHARLIE is always smiling. He has more than enough reasons to be happy. He's got his own business, pays no rent, and he's a tax evader.

He gazes at his customers. They're the picture of health. They congratulate him, joke with him, envy him. Fat Charlie comes up to Balboa, looks at his soapy hands and smiles.

"It's a good start," he says. "This is how I began twenty-five years ago, just like you, washing dishes in a restaurant. Follow my example, boy: waiter, cook, manager, owner of a chain of restaurants: Balboa's.

A young millionaire: you invest in Wall Street; buy a Greek island; get married a few times, only to models or movie stars; have daughters whose love affairs will turn into scandals; appear in magazines where your private life fills the gossip columns; rub elbows with royalty in the swankiest casinos in the world. You get old: you retire so you can enjoy your golden years vacationing, always with one eye on your investments, giving the final OK.

You die without leaving a will, in a Las Vegas hotel where you are the largest stockholder. A hundred fake wills turn up, along with a hundred pretenders to your inheritance. Hollywood's latest heartthrob plays your life on the screen. From a safety deposit box called "Paradise," you'll be having a grand time playing cards with God.

Only in America, baby. What more could a man want in life?

With his hands in the soapy water, washing the endless mounds of plates, Balboa stretches, and every once in a while manages to get a look at the legs of the fair-haired Mary Ann.

Considerations Regarding the Fair-Haired Mary Ann

THOSE HIPS OF HERS, wriggling in a pink miniskirt and white apron. She's the fair-haired Mary Ann, in sensible shoes and short sleeves. Bare arms and legs. She smiles with white teeth and subtle marks like semicolons on her pallid cheeks. She calls you Darling like you truly were her darling, like she's never said it to anyone else, like she's producing this stale cliché for the very first time when she says it to you. She's so slick that she totally convinces you she loves you. Bacon, eggs and apple pie are seldom as delectable as her eyes of Texas blue.

Maybe her hands have washed too many dishes. Maybe her feet have walked down too many roads: that's why they have traces, restless tracks. But the details don't matter. You forget them when she says Darling and writes words on her order pad that only she and the cook recognize, through that age-old pact between cooks and waitresses, consecrated in olden times when fog and sickness covered the earth and when powerful lords (ibm

Ismaelita was the ultimate peacock, the Mother of all Snottiness, the Creme de la Creme, Vanity Incorruptible. She wouldn't talk to any of the children; no one could bring her down off her cloud. She only had eyes for me. Although she asked me to lend her money and never paid it back, I was certain of her love.

99

coca cola xerox itt) dwelt in castles that guarded them from the fearsome foe Thirdworld, that ubiquitous, omnipresent bad guy.

Mary Ann, blonde and scrawny, carries plates smiling pleasing and at the end of the afternoon she adds up her tips to compute the shameful tax that—no getting around it—you have to pay.

In Which Our Hero Chooses the Profession that Will Define Him, and Which Will Engender this Remarkable, Not to Mention Interesting, Tale

AFTER FINISHING HIGH SCHOOL Balboa decided to be a conquistador. It was a very popular career back in the 16th century.

Most of his friends had already taken off for the Conquest. Some of their parents were against it because of the danger, but it was impossible to keep their kids from leaving. New World adventure was full of all those legends that you only see in the comic books: horrible dragons, adorable maidens, bull-dyker Amazons.

"I want to be a conquistador," Balboa said to his dad.

"That's fine with me. Just remember: men are always looking for something without knowing what it is."

"I want to be a conquistador," Balboa said to his mom.

"Why not a doctor, Son? Or a lawyer?"

As he packed his bags before setting sail for the New World, he dreamed about battles, about wars that filled him with honor and triumph. It was already in the cards. The moving hand was writing his proverbial destiny on the blackboard: the Conquest of New Spain was already over. What it needed now were bureaucrats—people to shuffle the archival documents, file them in alphabetical order and write summaries.

The tale was about to begin:

Amid the markets and canals
of the great city of Mexicco-Tenochtitlan,
smack on the corner where nowadays Dolores Street...

Balboa's Observations About Blondes in General and Legs in Particular

THERE'S SOMETHING ABOUT blondes," Balboa mused, "that I have not seen in Indian or Peninsular women. Despite their pale complexions, which often turn me off, one forgets all that because of the fine, soft sierra of down that covers their legs and makes them shine—Oh Jesus, flash!—like they're giving off their own glow when the sun or bright light hits them.

"And the fair-haired Mary Ann may not be beautiful, nor seem well fed, poor thing. But when she steps out of her pantyhose—Sweet Jesus Mary Mother of God—and her luminous mantle is exposed, it's time to place my heart on her lap, as though I were a human sacrifice and she a goddess of stone.

Questionnaire

The conquistador in love with the fair-haired Mary Ann?

For real?

Where's she from? Where in the world did she come from?

In love with two women?

Were we fools? Were we outsiders? Did we live lives that were not of our making?

The blonde in love with our hero Balboa?

Oh, really?

Where did he come from? What brought him here? Why now?

Loving someone else when the whole world thinks you're incapable of love?

Were we fools or did we let ourselves be carried away by the high tide that pulled us farther and farther into the deepness of the deep blue sea, pushing us toward the horizon, that line that marks the end of the earth—and the end of this novel?

In Which He Thinks Helplessly About Certain Affairs of the Heart

YOU. Hey you. Hey you! What, tell me—what do you know about love?

This screw this wave this trampoline this artichoke.

You! Hey! Tell me. Tell me! What do you know about love?

That greed for it, that yen for it, that stupefied thinking and thinking about it, that never stopping it.

It comes, I guess, from some deep darkness.

The heart? The brain? The pancreas? The left lung?

I don't wanna don't wanna oh please oh no.

She comes, comes walking and here you are like an idiot wanting to see her thinking about her as though she were the goddamned umbilicus of the moon, forever white forever in the middle with a—oh shit please no.

And being with her, being with her is the essential moment the vital instant: when the world stops trembling, and being with one no being with the other is time that cannot be abolished, a calendar whose pages never fall to the floor never turn into something else never cause scandal.

You. Hey you! What…? What do you know about this stuff? Where does it come from how does it start?

She's the fair-haired Mary Ann. She's Florinda.

The world seems better but sometimes the world seems worse. Life is not so weighty, although sometimes life can drown us and life can do us in.

You. Hey you!

Screw. Wave. Trampoline. Artichoke.

I don't want her I don't want her but I do I want her so bad!

Balboa sitting in a lone chair in front of a table and a hot dog, thinking about these things (You! Hey you.), not coming to any conclusion because when it comes to these sorts of questions—as we all well know—you don't come you don't arrive you don't get near you don't understand you don't learn you don't know I don't know I don't know oh *what the hell* I don't know.

In Which He Discovers, Much to His Chagrin, Other Balboas in this Sad and Downcast Empire

BOUNDLESS SADNESS upon discovering that many conquistadors just like him live around here: travelers, adventurers, looking for fame and fortune via the same routes. He would run into them in the malls, on the sidewalks of the main shopping strips, in the train yards hiding from the Border Patrol. Only they could identify each other (the giveaway was their elegant style, their chivalrous manners). They never paused to greet each other.

Was that because they were ashamed of their status as conquered conquistadors?

Were they, perhaps, victims of a failure, of a grave deception?

Once I wanted to touch her hand but just then we passed her stop and she got off the bus. Damned Ismaelita!

Or could it be that the Northernish Empire, with its strength, its expanse, its immensity—that it had made them seem strange to themselves, had turned them into weird beings, less cheerful, less caring?

Balboa quickly realized that he wasn't supposed to say hello either when he saw them on the street. Not that it would have mattered if he did, since they would never have returned the greeting. And when he ran into them at a pool hall, which happened a lot, he had to fight his natural instinct to run up and embrace them. This was another land, and here the logic and brotherhood of the conquistador did not apply.

Little by little he came to understand this, and even ended up making conquistador friends with whom he never talked of his exploits, nor of the Mother Land.

It bears mentioning here: that although he adapted to these new customs, he never failed to feel a flutter in his stomach when he spotted some conquistadors. He never stopped suffering a twinge of sadness. He never ceased thinking that they were the only thing that tied him to the Conquest in these faraway lands to the North.

When All Is Said and Done, Out of Sight Really Is Out of Mind

BALBOA is nearsighted. But not in a way that glasses would help, not like that. The distance is making things blurry. Florinda's features—her dark face, for example—are taking on that fogginess which covers everything left behind.

In a dream, Balboa saw his beloved with another face, another personality, other feelings. When he woke up he wondered whether Florinda could have changed so that she was no longer insensitive or flighty or fickle. Even though he knew perfectly well that she had never been insensitive, flighty or fickle.

He yearned for a different Florinda, and never realized that distance was playing tricks on him, trying to warp his love.

Distance was mocking Balboa, tempting his heart, saying, "OK, let's see if your love can really stand up to a little pressure."

"When all is said and done, out of sight really is out of mind, and the moon will forever be a distant love…," Balboa concluded nearsightedly.

His restlessness became vast and categorical.

It chewed him up and spit him out.

Washing Dishes

*S*ATURDAY NIGHT: a steak, fries, salad and a beer.

Balboa, exploring his teeth with a toothpick.

Mary Ann, washing the dishes.

The conquistador muses: some people, when they wash their dishes, first soap them then rinse them.

Other people, when they wash their dishes, first they rinse then they soap.

When Mary Ann does her own dishes, she rinses and soaps at the same time.

Balboa would like to be one of fair-haired Mary Ann's foamy dishes.

"But am I in love with her?" he wonders.

A Letter to Conquistador Balboa

IN HIS DREAM, Balboa awakens, looks at the ceiling like he always does, then smiles and gets up to take a piss. He finds an envelope under the door. This is a surprise, because he's a little like the Colonel Nobody Writes To. Besides, he never sends letters. He tried to—to send a letter to Florinda. He thought he'd have a lot to say to her, but when he sat down in front of a blank piece of paper, not much came out.

"Since the time when last I saw thee, life hath not been the same. Branded is my heart by thy absence…"

In his dream, he opens the envelope and finds a letter:

In the year 6706 of the Julian Era, according to the 168th Calendar of the most ancient Galván. From an island called California.

My Good Conquistador Balboa:
Many moons have passed since you departed for the conquest with the sun at your back. Many moons, Balboa, and now in the North, the evenings still riffle over the reflection of the water. Nothing disturbs them: their colors continue to paint miracles upon the seagoing skin of my people.

111

Sitting here in the grass, I listen to the stepping of the wind, which—like you—would sap the strength from every journey. I listen to it and I think: it's a good empire, this one, with its plazas and markets. A good empire that you have conquered with the sword of your nearsighted eyes. Will you talk about it to your silver-armored friends? Will they believe you, Balboa?

Here, the palm trees sway, revealing borders within one's reach.

Here, regardless of arrivals or departures, the reflection of the dream stays the same.

Here, errant knight, the conqueror is conquered by the large eyes of my people. By women forged from metal and desire, from skin and from flames. For in our skin, Balboa, is found the secret of life.

Evening is falling, Traveler. Flocks of recollections graze the magical grass of the mirage. Are there schools of waves in your maritime empire? You are so far away that you could touch me. Will you do so, gentle Balboa?

In his dream, the Conquistador does not completely understand the letter.

He figures it has something to do with knighthood tales, like *Sergas de Esplandián* that he's been reading lately, or with a plate of enchiladas that didn't agree with him. He also figures that it must have been written by some woman who was neither Florinda nor Mary Ann.

In his dream, he imagines the author of the letter with a perpetual smile, a peaches-and-cream complexion, big lips, brown, wavy hair—nothing like Florinda or Mary Ann.

In his dream, he folds the letter and puts it back into the envelope with no return address.

…although she often reacts as if she were a child—the imagination continues—(she leaps joyfully, she has fun climbing trees), it surprises you to hear her meditating about the world, it excites you to know that she's more intelligent and introspective than you'll ever be.

In his dream, many pleasant aromas surround him and everything is in its place, the way it's supposed to be. But the alarm clock goes off at 6 A.M., and the letter is lost in that dusty part of memory that many people label the unconscious, and which others, with no compunction, call oblivion.

He Didn't Want to Go, Not Yet, But He's Back with Florinda on The Border of New Spain

WALKING DOWN THE STREET on the way to his job, thinking about Mary Ann's blue eyes, about her waitress outfit and about the Jergen's creme that she stroked on her legs when she got out of the bathtub, Balboa was surprised by a pair of beefy guards who handcuffed him and threw him in a van.

It was not yet time. He still had much to conquer. He attempted to explain this to the guards: he prevailed upon their masculinity, begged their indulgence, pleaded for their manly understanding of other things. Balboa didn't want to go back, not yet—but he journeyed again to New Spain, and having no choice in the matter, his thoughts returned to Florinda, to the slender, neatly dark and gleaming legs of his beloved F, with whom he would have to declare a truce and make some peace.

One time his Uncle Decorous told him: Be careful of the Border Patrol. They are hair-raising creatures, half-man and half-beast, gatekeepers of the Empire. They have but one mission in life— to check out what you look like, what color your skin is, and if it doesn't please them, to send you back to New Spain.

What Can I Tell Her, How Can I Explain So That She'll Believe There Is No One Like Her in the World—No Love So Wonderful, Nor Any So Amazing As My Love for Florinda, the Heroine of this Tale?

▼

I can't think of anything.

Good Manners

FLORINDA and Balboa at the New Oriental Cafe. She very serious, picking her fork through the broccoli, jicama and other indecipherable vegetables. He also very serious, digging into the Cantonese chicken, which works its magic, delighting his stomach.

"Well, I'm back," the Conquistador says. He wanted to tell her: "So many things have transpired. I have discovered an enormous world, a fabulous place, a land of opportunity, where a man can fill himself with riches, be a king, a god, be happy…" But nothing comes to mind.

"I don't like The Border," she says. "I don't like it."

"But there's so much stuff here. Have you seen everything?"

Balboa is worried. He senses a lack of trust in Florinda, a diminution of love, a sudden boredom, a sad ending.

He remembers the women who fall in love with conquistadors before they leave on their expeditions, and wait and wait for them until either they return or until learning of their death.

His beloved is not like those women.

His beloved is better.

He admires her.

For a few seconds, Mary Ann's legs hide out at the bottom of his memory.

When he came back to his aunt and uncle's house, Balboa felt that forgotten desperation to see Florinda again. He had returned to his True Love. There were no words for it. There would be no words when Florinda received him at the door with open arms. He decided simply to close his eyes and embrace her mightily. And to think: "Nothing can come between this love that I feel for thee."

But the person who opened the door was Aunt Onelia.

"Dost thou like it?" Balboa asks, referring to the food.

"No," F answers. "No."

She doesn't like the food.

Balboa tries to say, "I am a conquistador on the inside, not the outside. Appearances can be deceiving."

But this little declaration gets lost in a sip of tea. That's the problem with eating and thinking, eating and wanting to say something, eating and wanting to be sure of love. How can he reiterate to Florinda that for him she is the New World when his mouth is full of vegetables?

Balboa thinks: "If women were things you bought, you'd know how to take care of them and would always be sure of finding them in their place."

A lake of resentment surrounded the city of Florinda. To conquer her again, Balboa would have to build a brigantine to float across.

Could he see her, explain to her, convince her, so that once again she'd believe in his love?

Could she tolerate his absence again without feeling wounded, without carrying a cross, while he wrapped things up with the blonde Mary Ann?

When He's With Her,
When He's With Her

▼

she listens silently

she interrupts, whether she's indignant or satisfied

she's possessed of a vigorous, worrisome gravity

she's always smiling and making wisecracks

she talks of life and the cosmos; she ponders the fate of things, she worries about the wanton felling of trees

she lives for the moment; she looks to the world for happiness; she's read *I'm OK, You're OK*

she's a very practical shopper

she often spends a whole day bargain hunting at the mall; she buys things she doesn't need

she's bilingual

she's bilingual

she wears simple clothes: an Aztec blouse and sandals; she often goes barefoot at home; she combs her hair upward, into two buns that look like horns; she doesn't wear jewelry,

she doesn't dress in the latest styles; in fact, she mocks them, with wide, billowy skirts; she wears a lot of bracelets, and her carelessly combed hair recalls a time when everyone believed,

nor deck herself out in bright
colors, because to do so
"means you're carnal, a
woman of the world"

more than anything, in peace
and love

she offers me rest, peace: what
we're all looking for in life

she wakes me up, she shakes
me, she wants to take me
dancing: what we're all looking
for in life

she's conscientious, thoughtful, she doesn't do anything
without consulting me first
and understanding my opinion

she's impulsive; she acts on
instinct; if she feels like
shouting she shouts

But when I'm with her, when I'm with her, the two of them seem
like one person to me, like they were born from the same
mother—Siamese twins, separated at birth. And when I'm with
her, when I'm with her, I wish I were two men. Two: one here,
one there: two. I think that's called ubiquity.*

*The poet explains: "A philosophy which attempts to prove that one
subject, simultaneously, is able to love two others."

Farewell, Sweet Florinda

YOU ARE MY TRUE LOVE, sweet Florinda, you are forever, truly you are, but there are things (how can I explain this to you?) that are special in every man's life and one can do no less than surrender himself to them, to not let them go by because they may not come again, though one would not wish to hurt thee and one does not want to make thee think that time or distance has lessened our love and one does not wish to abandon thee like this, alone in this house but the whole thing isn't over and I can assure thee that it is not true, only an illusion, but I must live it, milady, I have to grab the chance now and go back to her so that later I'm not left hanging, unsatisfied, but you are my True Love, sweet Florinda, you are forever, truly you are and I hope for your understanding, although I have no words although it seems that I am angered, infuriated with thee but it's the worry the anxiety and I cannot find the words to explain to thee how I feel because how could you understand, it is confusion, total confusion and it would leave you thinking that thy love has ended and that Balboa is no longer in your heart that you're no longer in Balboa's heart, which isn't true I swear to you it's not true milady you are the world discovered in the sixteenth century, to which we must return because it is ours, and the rest hardly matters, since this time this city do not matter they are mere parentheses, easily forgotten and how do I tell you to pardon me, Florinda, but it is fate it is life's road it is a land inescapably conquerable urgently governable farewell sweet Florinda for I must go.

In the Supermarket

BETWEEN THE ROWS of vegetables detergents cereals canned food electrical appliances paper products deodorants, Mary Ann and Balboa push the shopping cart of their happiness. They fill it with necessities, with indispensable objects, basic utensils.

For a few seconds, the shopping cart is a cornucopia.

They both contemplate their happiness and smile.

Then, they look in their wallet.

And just as calmly as when they were filling their cart of happiness, they begin emptying it, returning things to where they belong.

They pay for their merchandise and go home with a single small shopping bag.

Balboa watches soberly at how Mary Ann undresses.

"But am I in love with her?" he wonders.

Why Should I Let You Go?

▼

an essay by Mary Ann Simpson

The oldest memory I possess is probably of my father lifting me up high and looking at me with his smiling face. It's funny that I remember him this way since he was not a man who smiled easily. Nevertheless, his image is clear in my head: his big smile, his pink face, his large body.

He liked The Platters. He liked their songs so much! That was the music in my home, night and day the same tunes: "Only You," "Smoke Gets in Your Eyes," "The Great Pretender"; and since he got fired from his job, he dedicated all his time to his little girl and to his well-worn records.

He would pick me up and dance with me. I would sleep in his arms and it was the best sleep--better than I've ever slept since.

How many years ago? In my memory I can't tell time.

My mother would get home from her job (she was a secretary), and she would complain to him that the house was never clean, that it looked like no one was taking care of it, that he should help out, do something. I think it was really hard for my father not to be able to find a new job because he was too old. And in the end, I think he convinced himself that he was of no use in this world. That was the worst thing: he had so many plans and didn't complete any of them. He wanted the best for me, and I don't know what he would think now, but I guess if he saw me he would sink into a deep depression. I'm nothing like what he dreamed of. He wanted me to study but I didn't. He wanted life to be good to me but that hasn't happened.

Why am I writing this to you since I just met you and my life probably doesn't mean much to you?

I'm writing to you because you can't read English.

I'm writing to you because you're asleep next to me now, and I would never tell you any of this.

I'm writing to you because I know you won't understand.

124

I'm writing because I have to. I mean, I have to do this essay as homework for Professor Spike, and it's a very boring class and I need to pass.

I didn't finish high school--you know? I didn't finish because I met a man who made me promises, and I believed him. He told me about a world good enough for us, where I wouldn't have to work, just take care of the house and the kids, watch them grow up. I thought it was the greatest thing. So we left for California. I left my father and mother behind and I haven't seen them since (someone told me he died eight years ago). So here I am, and you're asleep. Your naked back does not tell me what I seek to hear. No, and not even your words satisfy me. I don't really think we have anything in common, but here I was, by myself, and you, in the restaurant, telling me things I hadn't heard for ages except in the movies, and you reminded me of my father and
you reminded me of the guy who brought me to California by promising me the world. You haven't made any promises, you haven't made plans, but I'm sure that sooner or later you will, just as sure as the wind blows the leaves. That's how life is, and I'll believe you. Or maybe I won't. On second thought, maybe

I'll decide it's time for you to leave. I'll decide. Me. But it's not that easy, darling. Not that easy. I don't like being by myself. I don't like to pick up a book and read (although sometimes I do). I don't like to paint my nails or spend hours in front of the TV. I can't do it. I prefer your words, even though you don't have much to say, and you tell me about things I do not understand and never will.

I don't love you, but actually I do.

I love your presence, your naked back. I love the odd way you say gracias in the morning when I make breakfast, in a way I've never known and which seems to come from another time. I love how you're not modern, that you're antique.

I guess I would hate your absence. But I'll let you go, you'll go, and I'll go back to my world at the restaurant and the night school, hoping that Professor Spike will give me good grades and explain to me that this isn't an essay, that I should have dealt with a specific subject and I should have been more creative.

Professor Spike makes me laugh, too.

Then why am I writing to you?

And why like this?

I would never tell you what I'm writing right now, and to me it seems more fair that if any-one sees it, it should be my professor--don't you think?--with that way he has of explaining things to me like I was a five-year-old child.

Maybe I was five when my father lifted me up with The Platters and his unfulfilled life. Maybe.

That was the only time I've ever been a queen, and I liked it--I have to admit it--I liked being a queen, at least during those moments with The Platters and my father's strong arms holding me high.

Queen of Something, whatever it is.

I'm sorry, Professor Spike.

I'll do better next time.

I promise.

ns pump
o schools
op benefits

rs are striking
illions of dollars
high schools.
panies are right
ut the money
oper, Pepsi and
pay school
ikrolling new
unding salaries
achers.

it appears to be
hool athletics
cover travel
uy uniforms and
t's in it for the
s? Advertising
e agreements to
on campus.

example, has
ment that could
an $4 million to a
district during the
oft drinks sold
at school-
ave to be Dr.
. The company
recognition on
d in game
contracts rarely
glance in the big-
professional and
ut how far will
ite sponsorship
consider to be
sports in its
eren't for the
ls, we never
red into an
iis," said the
uperintendent.
need driven."
about $100,000
and products.
od chain, awards

The Holy Majesty Fan Club Invites You to Their Annual Get-Together

The lofty and all-powerful, the most excellent princess, the very Catholic Grande Dame, Lady Doña Isabella.

The "Amamus Tantum Reginam" Queen of Spain Fan Club, Inc., publicly announces its annual get-together to commemorate the birthday of Her Most Holy and Catholic Majesty, Doña Isabella. During said event, applications will be accepted from prospective new members, acts of charity and contrition will be presented, and lives of heretics condemned to be burned at the stake will be spared (as long as and as soon as they accept the True Faith).

The gathering will feature an appearance by His Excellency the Duke of Gandía, who will proclaim the traditional missive by which her Highest and Holy Majesty honors us and gives thanks in the name of the Spanish crown. Likewise, it will feature an appearance by the bish-

(continued on page 8, Column 4)

Taxes

Lawmakers t
limit the numl
times a home'
can be assesse
to limit the in
in appraised p.
values.

In November
will be asked
increases in p
value should b
capped at 10 pe
a year. Homeo
would also be
allowed to defe
property tax
payments if val
rose more than
percent, but the
would pay 8 pe
interest to do so

Since 1995 the
Governor has s
rising property
rates and prope
values threaten
ownership in t
state. He said t
state's healthy
economy, the
approved tax
increased state
funding for edu
could take the
pressure off ri
local school-ta
He added that
people want m
be done, they w
have to make th
known to electe
officials.

The constituti
amendment ap
Saturday raise
minimum hor
property-tax
exemption by

PART FOUR

The Moon Will Forever Be a Distant Love

when love makes up its mind
the walls turn into sand

—VICENTE QUIRARTE

Apocryphal-Nostalgic Chapter That Perhaps Should Have Appeared in Part One of this Novel

BEING YOUNG and in love (or at least covered with that spark, that chimney, that café au lait that they call love), B and F had decided to get to know each other as soon as possible.

They went into one of those cafes that had sprouted up everywhere in the capital of New Spain. The time had come to set their sights on ancestral lineages and cosmogonies.

Their eyes asked: What were you like as a child, my fair-skinned my dark-skinned one how do you live now do you like movies fruit the smell of the sea of the woods walking without boots without sandals through the fresh, cool mornings of Madrid Tenochtitlan?

They yearned to share their history and her eyes listened listened as his spoke spoke.

Florinda, being considerate, did not wish to interrupt him, but the Spaniard spoke so enchantingly that she had to cut him off—OK, that's enough!—and the conquistador prudently played his cards close to his chest. Then F's eyes spoke spoke while Balboa's listened listened.

Through the cafe passed childhood and youth, discoveries and disillusionments.

The waitresses went back and forth, filling coffee cups adding up checks. "So this is love?" they asked themselves. Interrogatories and responses? Is this the proper way to do it, according to the manuals and instruction sheets?

The waitresses didn't know.

Balboa and Florinda, their eyes a vast silence, stopped talking listening and merely looked saw contemplated. Assaulted by drowsiness, startled, their hands entwined, B and F, wide-eyed, decided they'd done enough—that they finally knew each other!—and they paid the check.*

---

* The poet adds: "Who said that I willed this separation, this living without you?"

Men, Men

▼

Barbie Doll: They're beautiful, gorgeous. When I see the handsomest ones walking around I want to run up and hug them.

Sufferella: At times they're our punishment, at times our just reward. But oh! these days it's so hard to find an honest one. For a lot of girls like me, life goes by in solitude.

La China: I don't like guys who are wet behind the ears. I like the ones who've been around, so there's no hassles later on. If they decide to split, I'll cut out first.

Florinda: It used to be that I liked thinking about only one, but now I think about *them*, about several. Could they all be like the first one? I'd like one with a good heart, one who doesn't lose his niceness as the years go by.

Big City Girl: As long as he's not a chilango, anyone will do.

A Boy Like All the Rest, Passing By and Checking Her Out, Meanwhile She Can't Decide Can't Decide

H E'S A BOY like all the rest and he works in the maquiladora.

He comes out from the office area with a pencil and notepad. He passes by Florinda. He looks at her he leaves he comes back he returns he looks at her. He goes back to the office.

He's a boy like all the rest.

"He's really big. He's got a nice smile," Barbie Doll says.

Florinda looks at him as though instead of a boy, he was a tree on a hot day; she could sit beneath his shade and relax.

Two hours later: the boy comes back and looks at Florinda as though she was a sunny corner where he could shield himself from the cold.

Is It Sadness Is It a Whirlwind on a Hot Afternoon Is It Sweat Is It Sadness?

Soldering iron melt solder, solder solder circuits.

"Make your move," China says to her.

Soldering iron melt solder, solder solder circuits.

"I just can't. I can't make the first move, China."

"Don't make him suffer," sobs Sufferella.

After three weeks, the boy stops looking at her.

"See, what did I tell you!" China says.

Stuck in the Corner of a Shoe Store

THIS TIME she doesn't get together with her girl friends; she leaves them on their own to eat pizzas and get fat. She walks through the business districts, she gazes at the movie billboards, she buys a pack of cigarettes then throws them away because she doesn't know how to smoke.

"It's easy," La China had said, her mouth full of smoke. "You just suck it in and blow out."

Florinda buys a pair of shoes that she contemplates before the mirror. She looks at them. She looks at the mirror. She looks at them. An urge to weep wets the world. It's the ugly shoes it's the terrible times it's the soldering iron it's the solder.

Florinda buys another pair of shoes.

She turns into an addict. She tells no one. Not Barbie Doll or Sufferella or La China or Big City Girl. Her shoe-aholism is Anonymous.

Hi. My name is Xóchitl. I buy shoes.

In this world of footwear, it's impossible to avoid them: patent leather high heels low heels suede boots huaraches sandals.

Her salary squandered on shoes every payday. She comes home with huge bags. Aunt Onelia gets suspicious:

"What you're doing is wrong," she tells her. "You must be strong."

But Florinda isn't weak; she just needs shoes: of plastic fake leather fake plastic. SHOES! Cheap and dear. No matter. Men's women's. Horrible colors cute colors. No matter. For Florinda, shopping for shoes has become an obligation, a civic patriotic duty like paying taxes like stepping up to the precinct booth and voting.

Her room with its boxes everywhere.

"Oh, Florinda," sighs Onelia.

To make a long story short: this goes on for a couple of months until one day, starting in the fall (when the garden is dirty with leaves and the maquiladora awash in dollar bills) the boy who's like all the rest starts insisting again.

She's Looking at Him and What Happens is that the Whole Thing Starts Again, Like So Many Things Do in Life, and Like They Do in This Tale

▼

Her: Well, I'm looking at him looking at me; well, he's not saying anything to me. Moving his fork in the beans. I keep quiet. I stay mum. So what else? He's not bad looking. He stares at me insistently but he'd better not or I'll smash him. I'll raise my hand and I'll smash his face in because of that way he has of staring that's not terrible but it's deep, obstinate. Calm down, Xóchitl. You're overreacting. The speaker will squawk again and it'll be time to go back to work. It didn't do him any good to ask me if he could sit next to us girls and then stare at me like I'm the Atayde Circus and don't overreact goddamn Sufferella, don't start crying.

Him: Well, I'm looking at her and she's not talking to me. Moving her fork in the beans. I keep quiet; can't think of anything to say. For example: telling her she's pretty, that I like the chocolate color of her hands: the palms aren't as dark as the backs. I've already felt her voice and it's enchanting; it sounds just like a carpenter's tender hammering—yes!—she repeats her words words words words and I think I'm sweating and she's getting annoyed. If only I were more of a man: Pedro Infante, Luis Aguilar, Jorge Negrete, Frank Sinatra: Strangers in the Night, Exchanging Glances…what would my Stranger think of me? What should I say to her explain to her offer her? Dear Miss Lonely Hearts: What should I do? How to explain my attraction to her if there's no tequila in my hand and I don't even know how to let out a hearty yell like Pedrito did in the cantinas when he was feeling bad about Blanca Estela. Maybe she likes cumbias?

Her: He keeps looking looking at me. He watches me. He snoops around like I'm some kind of I-don't-know-what, I-don't-know-how-much, and I don't like it, don't like it. Enough already! Make him say something, something, something, make him explain to me ask me out. Maybe he likes cumbias? I'm looking at La China who's looking at me looking, and she closes one eye. Shut up China; I've got enough problems with Balboa the one who left without saying a word and then shoes shoes shoes in my house like dandelions that simply multiply in the air and the wind. Do me a favor and don't stare at me, Barbie Doll; I've got enough going on with this Joe Blow who's staring at me like he wants to say something but he's not saying anything. Should I make the first move? Hell no. I'm not starting.

Him: I'm no Fred Astaire, Florinda, I'm no Gene Kelly. I can't even dance to simple songs that go one-two-three one-two-three. But I'd like to ask you out. To tell you a little about the movie studios in Churubusco and Hollywood, which is the only thing I know about. You're staring at me. Ayyayyayyyy! You keep staring at me, that's great. Will you be patient with me? Yesterday in front of the mirror, everything turned out OK: "Florinda, I'd like to take you out dancing"* (me like Clark Gable), and you, in front of my mirror, were saying: "No problem, pick me up at six" (like Vivien Leigh); then I come for you in my late model car (which I don't have), elegantly dressed, the best after-shave (Henry Fonda); you take my arm and at the dance hall we glide through the cumbia, a cumbia without end on this planet (Bette Davis in a red dress); later we live happily in front of my mirror with seventeen children, all of them the image of you (my beloved Betty with the big eyes). Florinda...

---

*The poet muses: "Such pleasant madness it would be, dancing with you to the magical beat of an old serenade."

They Chat for the First Time and Nothing Is Like It Was Supposed to Be

FLORINDA…"

"What."

"The beans are good, aren't they?"

"Kind of burned."

"You're right. They're burned."

"I don't like them."

"Me neither."

"Want to go dancing?"

"What kind of dancing?"

"Cumbias."

"Cumbias!"

"Afterwards I'll take you out for pizza."

"No way, not pizza."

"Chinese."

"That's worse than pizza."

"Tacos."

"Maybe."

As though announcing the end of a fight at an empty coliseum, the bell says it's time to go back to work.

140

To Go Dancing or Stay in His Arms, Listening to the Soft Melody of His Breathing?

SO, WHAT NOW?

Do we make eyes at each other do we get lovey-dovey?

Do I like your teeth do you like my skirt?

Will we compose festive, tortured, eloquent songs?

Will you make promises?

Will I promise what I already promised already will I say will you say words I already said you already said?

Love vicissitude heartfelt nostalgia cockroach in the heart walking through ventricles and auricles?

Will you be the one to fill up my photo album?

Don't you know how to dance you've got two left feet two right hands don't you know how to dance?

Are you an explorer a conquistador I follow the feint of your voice your arms your not knowing how to dance talk sing. Or should I keep quiet exploring you conquering you as if I were the one who'd come from a faraway place across the sea and it was your culture (and not mine) that was disrupted, unsuspecting, warlike?

Anger?

Don't you think there's anger/sadness that I'm new to this stuff

141

that I haven't lived through a love that I (like other women) thought was complete thoughtful eternal engaging?

Will I love you like the pillar of a house we've not yet built but where you'll be the foundation the walls windows the electrical wiring that illuminates the hallways of my entrance?

Believe in you?

You're really getting hung up on this guy you just met, Xóchitl— What's His Name? Is it just because he says/does the same things some other guy (Other Guys) has probably said/done to you before?

Repeating repeating life goes by repeating like a stutter of life stut-stut-ter-ter-rr-rr?

Florinda, are you insisting all over again, without thinking of how little time how short the wait till the end of this feature film?

Are you insisting all over again as if you didn't have the other dude on your forehead like a mark of ashes not even in the depths of your thoughts but still between your eyes like Ash Wednesday, please?

All over again, then?

All over again?

All over again.

Mechanics

AYBE it was the psst-psst from the mechanics, workers at El Pocho's Auto Shop across the street from her house, that convinced Aunt Onelia that despite her Indianness, Florinda wasn't an ugly woman—far from it.

With their greasy clothing and nudie-girl pin-ups, they were the best connoisseurs of feminine beauty. Onelia had seen how they looked with disgust at Spanish Peninsular women with fine thighs and long legs: they were too picky for that type. On the other hand, there was never a time when Florinda went out shopping or to work that the mechanics hadn't come outside the garage with their psst-pssts and their eyes glued to her niece-in-law's unselfconscious walk, to her slender, always bare legs, to her round little shoulders and her upper arms that were hardly even marred by vaccination scars. The mechanics would leave their transmissions and carburetors, their spark plugs and brake pads to stand in the door looking at Florinda walking her walk and the subtle swaying of her hips (psst-psst) until, haughtily (ignoring them like some very dark Empress Carlotta or like an Indian Queen of Sheba) she disappeared around the corner.

And the mechanics, smiling, happy, smelling like gasoline, would go back to their transmissions, their carburetors, spark plugs and brake pads; to their nudie pin-ups (with enormous knockers psst-psst) that were stuck to the walls of the shop like effigies of the Immaculate Conception, benefactress to all those imprisoned by love or by lust.

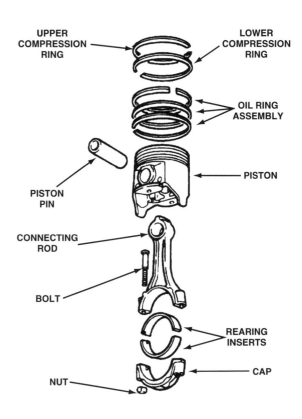

The Aunt Tells Her Story, the Only Important One, About Boldness and Resignation, While She Watches Florinda Pack Her Suitcases and Leave Without So Much as a Goodbye, With the Old Refrigerator, and Of Course She's Not Even Listening

▼

Shall I tell thee about my husband?

Decoroso has been taking off for a long time, and sometimes it's days before he comes back. Before, he had things to tell me: he would talk about his job, his hopes, about having a family. This was when we'd just gotten married.

Shall I tell thee what The Norteño says?

He talks to me about other women. He brings fashion magazines. He shows me photographs. He smiles. He adds: "I know all these models and none are like you." I don't let him come in, of course. I'm a married woman. I look at him through the fence. I look at his eyes and silently tell him about another world that could be ours. Sadly, it cannot be.

Shall I tell thee what my husband was like back then?

Short and strong, an accountant's assistant. Always whistling, always with a song on his lips. I miss that Decoroso who's been left behind. I miss the long walks, holding hands. I miss the rain that soaked us and made us run home. I miss how we used to cook together. Oh, the mess we made! That oh-so-slow way he had of washing the dishes, like he was going through our whole life story while he soaped and rinsed. It all ended with an abruptness I didn't understand. One Decoroso was left behind. The one who had hopes, yearnings, who lived for me and lived with me—he disappeared.

Shall I tell thee again about The Norteño?

He comes by every day, friendly, with his photos of gorgeous women. I want to hold him, to run away with him, but we each have to choose our road in life: so I put my hand in his* and calmly said goodbye. I showed him that I'm a lady; and he, sad gentleman, went away down the same street he'd come on. I hear his steps vanishing in the distance.

Shall I tell thee what I think now?

There are no other worlds, Florinda, only this one. There are no other lives for you to live over again in and make up for everything. God forgive me for what I'm saying. But take a chance, Florinda. It's now or never. Thou must lead thine own conquest. When the time was ripe I didn't do it, and life passed me by.

---

*The poet interrupts: "No one, not even the rain, has such tiny hands."

For Rent:

Fifth-floor Apartment, Centrally Located, to Single Woman Trying to Make a Life, to Put it Back Together Without Help Because Life and Buildings Possess the Cleansing Rhythm of Oblivion (Two Bedrooms Kitchen Living Room Bathroom Dining Room) or At Least That's What the Landlord with the Big Mustache and the Gray Hair Said to Convince Florinda

"Ugh, Ugh!!" Sufferella complained as she helped move the refrigerator with Big City Girl and La China.

Tragedy, dreadful tragedy: Barbie Doll broke a fingernail.

Sometimes it's better to live alone and depend on yourself. To distance yourself from your memories. It's better that way. The memories stay behind, along with the first words you ever read and the first flavors you tasted. Far from the present.

The current project is to get the moving done and start living in the fifth-floor apartment.

From the window, she rules over the avenue: the intersection of automobiles and people. From here to there is uncertainty. Across the street, other buildings much like hers line up and light up as night falls.

Now you can see the neighbors:

The family in the building right across the street: dad, mom, grandmother and two teenage girls who get ready every morning to go to high school. One of them dances in front of the mirror. The other, more serious, prepares her next day's lessons. On the door is a U2 poster: *Achtung Baby*.

In the other fifth-floor apartment, a blonde woman stands by the window every afternoon from six to seven, looking out the window. Would it be too much to speculate? No one comes. The woman makes her food and eats, going up to the window every once in a while. She smokes a cigarette or sometimes two, but never more than that. A little girl plays near her.

On the first floor of another building. So late at night that it's the wee hours, a man comes up and knocks at the back window. A woman opens the window, saying that she wasn't expecting him (a lie); he says he was just passing by and didn't really intend to see her (a lie), it's just that the other nights (yesterday, the day before yesterday) have been so full of meaning that one would not want to stop coming. Sooner or later, he will stop coming.

"Loneliness is a bitch," La China says, sweating.

"You'd better not move again, you damn chilanga," says Big City Girl.

"Oh God," says Barbie Doll.

"Ugh, ugh," says Sufferella.

Balboa Returns as Though He'd Just Left, As If Out of Sight Wasn't Out of Mind, As If Love Was as Reliable as an Old Volkswagen

COMING BACK isn't difficult; it's just leaving in reverse. Balboa has done it, cautiously turning his steering wheel, turning on his lights, carefully checking the road: the trail of crumbs that he left from the beginning in case of emergency.

Going away was necessary. It was his destiny. It had been foretold in the cards, in the palm of his hand, in the stars. Conquistadors travel, but they return. That's the way History is: going far away from the people you love, having adventures, doubting, experiencing temptations and returning at the end of the trip to praises worthy of heroes. Perhaps it's hard to understand for someone who's not a conquistador or a Spaniard, but it's part of life: the series of events

I look for her in an old class photo: Anibel, Ricardo Gil, Gaby, Miguel Angel, Ivón Solomón are there; but Ismaelita is not. Could it be that she was sick that day?

arranged by God on the march of Time. What can I do but accept these divine plans with humility? Is it really so hard to understand? That's the way we conquistadors are, and Florinda will

149

have to accept it the way I accept her dark skin and brown eyes.

But what if she doesn't?

What if she refused to? What if I showed her my birthmarks, my palm, my tea leaves, my astrological chart, and even then she still doesn't understand?

No doubt about it, she's an intelligent person. But at times, women get ideas that get in the way of natural logic. For example: if I had told her "the sky is violet," she would look out the window to correct me: "the sky is blue," and no matter how hard I tried to explain it to her, to tell her that violet is a pleasing color that comes from passion, she would insist that "the sky is blue it's blue," and there would be no way of getting her off that: her blue versus my violet.

Here are the possible outcomes:

a) F forgives him because she understands what is explained above;

b) F does not forgive him because she refuses to understand and B pretends to be offended until she reconsiders;

c) F does not forgive him because she knows that what's described above is an ice cube left out in the heat;

d) B reverts to emotional blackmail;

e) B falls back on memories of happier times;

f) B gets down on his knees and implores her (which is behavior unfitting for a conquistador);

g) B makes up a story about Sirens and magic incantations that caught him in a spell; and

h) Both blame the times we live in: times of social change and endless wars. How is it possible to believe in love after seeing the newscasts?*

---

*The poet reconsiders: "If I married the daughter of my washerwoman, maybe I'd be happy."

150

Words that Might Have Happened, But Since Life Goes By in Silences, Looks and Gestures, None of This Got Said

$\int$O NOW WHAT?"

"So now what?"

"It's been a long time."

"A long time."

"What do you want from me?"

"Understanding."

"Understanding of what?"

"Of life: this blooming miasma that spreads this divine dialogue, this poorly focused dusk.

"Life isn't what it used to be."

"We started off badly."

"We're still doing badly."

"Vicissitudes, F, everyday life, advertising and marketing. It's the march of History it's Progress it's the Manifest Destiny that we all carry in our pancreas.

"Manifest Destiny. In other words: Indians fuck over Indians, Spaniards fuck over Indians; Indians and mestizos fuck over Spaniards; mestizos fuck over Indians, and mestizos fuck over each other?"

"That's the story of our country."

"What you mean *our*, keemosabee?"

"Progress."

"The massacre at Cholula, at Tlatelolco, in Chiapas; the death of Moctezuma and Cuauhtémoctzin; the slow extermination of the indigenous peoples from 500 years ago until now?"

"Recriminations?"

"Don't use big words on me, Balboita."

"Don't misanthropize, Effie."

"Wanna fight? Wanna go three rounds, no time limit, shave off your hair and your dignity if you lose?"

"I wish for world peace, and to stand on the beach and contemplate the sea until a dolphin leaps up, or a whale."

"White man speak with forked tongue."

"OK, OK, Florinda. What do you say we wipe the slate clean and start all over again?"

"Just like a guy: wipe it clean and start over."

"Just like a dame: always bearing a cross."

"You're a mean, groveling Spanish bastard."

"You, on the other hand, are a beautiful Indian who has been terribly wounded by this vile man who deserves nothing, but who asks for, hopes for, has need for one, just one, of your pardons."

"Even your voice has changed. You're not the same person I saw for the first time and who I (silly me) thought I was in love with. You don't say *thou* to me anymore, you don't lisp, you're not the same."

"And you, my love, no longer repeat yourself; you've eliminated that unnerving little detail from your low-class speech. No doubt you also know how to open the corn flakes."

"I open them the same, I open them the same."

"At heart we're the same; that's what I'm trying to explain to you, and that heart is what united us, what mixed, linked, unified, stuck together, stitched, combined…"

"Lots of synonyms, lots of synonyms."

"*Roget's Thesaurus.*"

"You can't even be original with *this* stuff."

"I'm bound to have at least one virtue that will make you consider getting back together, kind F: there's hair growing on my formerly hairless pecs; I have a better singing voice; I've been thinking of taking oboe lessons at the music academy. I would do it all for you, so that you'd take me back in your life. I would do it for your forgiveness, for the birds of the earth who fly at all hours over my memory of you."

"Poor Balboa."

"Forgive me, forgive me. Oh merciful forgiveness."

"The thing is, we're not the same as before. Don't you understand? Time distance indecision new encounters life in general."

"We're not the same? Of course we are."

"Not anymore. Not anymore," says Florinda. She closes the door, takes a few steps and turns on the television.

Stuck in the Corner of a Cantina Feeling Lost as He Imbibes Industrial-Strength Quantities of Alcohol and the Earth Begins to Turn Around the Heavens and Sing

LIKE A FOOL like a clown like a wild onion like tripe á la madrilène like a drunk the morning after like a dead man brought back to the living, I cannot stop thinking of you," thinks Balboa as he listens to the tortured songs of Agustín Lara:

> *Listen: I tell you in secret that I love you true*
> *I follow your steps though you don't want me to*
> *I feel your life more, the more you leave me*
> *No person, no thing makes my breast forget thee*

So, Memory, for Once Dwell on Constancy; from Inconstancy's Hold Let Nature Be Free

FLORINDA is examining the scar on her foot. It's a wound that healed quickly, one caused long ago by a bit of broken glass. She turns on the TV. The news comes on: the news is the same old thing. She reads the newspaper— her horoscope predicts a trip to exotic places. Yeah sure, what else is new?

Should she go back to the city she yearns for? It's too soon. Her memory has still not wilted; she still finds in it "those streets half of water, half of earth, those streets that you cross and wherever the water crosses there are bridges." She leaves her memories alone. She leafs through *The Second Sex*, a book she just bought that barely grabs her interest. She muses about the state of the world we live in. Is five hundred years nothing? Right, nothing. She starts to feel sad, and begins the letter that she's put off writing for so long:

Dear Auachtli:

Time flies and I still haven't put this letter in the mail box.

There is so much to say to you, so much to tell you, but the

problem is that you don't know how to read, and that has
kept me from writing. Well anyway, someone will read you
this letter and you will know that your little girl is well,
and that life has tested me but that

She starts over.

Dear Friend:

Yes, I really am that hare who leaps from field to field.
I truly am that nostalgic woman who is thinking of you.

The third version gets it just right.

Auachtli, My Friend:

So much to tell you and so little time. Do you still believe in me?
Do you still believe in your little girl? I have grown so much
inside. I am so big inside. My clothes fit me, but I am big inside.
Do you understand? I wish I could have you by my side
and speak to you from my heart. I would like to look at
your round face that talks to me and worries about me.
I miss your laugh, your strong laughter, your laugh.
Sometimes I listen to songs that speak of you and dad
and mom. Sometimes I listen to songs that ask me
to go back home. For now I'm not returning, Auachtli.
My plans have changed. I am not on The Border for the
same reasons. The people I hang out with are not the same
ones as before. I don't want to go into it.
I think there are things in this New World that I must do.

156

Which things I don't know, but in due time I'll be doing them.
I have met a boy who talks to me about the movies and tells
me things I never dreamed of. I am having feelings that
I thought a person could only feel one time. It's amazing,
Auachtli. Why didn't you tell me about this? You, who know
everything, should have told me that one can feel and then
feel again. I had no idea. He wants to come into my life like a
tree that falls down despite all efforts to keep it standing.
It's good that he wants to, but I tell him, "Eat chocolate, lad,
eat chocolate" and sometimes he understands but sometimes he doesn't. I really am that hare who hops from field to
field. I really am that nostalgic woman. Today is my birthday,
Auachtli, and my friends are about to arrive with presents,
best wishes and pizzas (have you ever eaten pizza?).
The boy will get here later on tonight. Should I allow him to
come inside this building that is my life? Throw your kernels
of corn and tell me. Put Xochiquétzal, the Goddess
of Love, on her head and tell me what
happens. Meanwhile, I will be living and
leaping from field to field,
Auachtli, my friend...

No.

Florinda decides
to put off the letter.

157

Balboa Shouting From the First Floor to Florinda, "Open the Door! Open the Door!" As Though Instead of a Conquistador He Was an Out-of-Tune Mariachi Serenading a Sagacious Woman

OPEN THE DOOR, F, open the door! I'm the same conquistador the same person your guttural sounds the measuring tape you'll use to calculate our future! I am breakfast served on the table of your happiness, the car heating up in the garage of our history, the curtains which, every morning when you open them, illuminate the center of our destiny! There's no better film soap opera photograph or postcard! It's all here, sweetness—life, time; the world's clocks stop, and the traffic and the soccer games! Open the door, F, open up because I want to come into the condominium of your days, enter the room of your words to warm myself in the bed of your accommodating arms! At least listen to me, woman, look out the window a little and contemplate this man who dresses and talks like a conquistador. If thou shouldst wisheth it, I can tell thee

Ismaelita, Ismaelita, where have you gone?

158

what thou wantsts, Florinda! Look upon this poor guy from the 16th century who has come to shout at you to call you tell you how much love he has for thee! Don't you feel a little pity for me? Just a little bit? Compassion pity commiseration? The night is too night and the cold too cold to sleep alone in the park. Besides, the mosquitoes, those terrible mosquitoes. Yecchh! Five floors is nothing, out of sight is not out of mind. The moon far away, the stars. My little Indian, have mercy. Get with it: the moon will always be a distant love, F, but there's no reason ours has to be that way!

("I Think I Should Even Give Her Credit for this Insanely Heroic Habit of Talking to Myself.")

THE NEIGHBOR LADIES heard him. They saw him through the windows of their apartments. They called the cops.

Florinda had gone out to the supermarket.

The Inevitable End of the Novel Arrives Just When Nobody (or Everybody) Was Expecting It

IT'S NIGHTTIME.

You cross the street with seven shopping bags. You're thinking about how the vegetables should have been divided up better so the bags wouldn't weigh so much. "Ugh, ugh," Sufferella would have said. But what can you do? You're just across the street from your building when you see him. Who? The Devil. Nahual. Calm down, Xóchitl, get a hold of yourself. It's just him: your ex.

You surprise yourself wondering if your hair looks nice: how silly.

What should you say to him. Should you greet him? Throw him a "hi" like it was a coin tossed into the air?

"Hi," you say, but not to him.

"Tomorrow," you predict but you don't say anything to him.

"All over again," you insist, but you don't say anything to him.

He's looking towards your apartment, his lips twisted with irritation.

"What's up?" you get up the nerve to ask, surprising him.

He looks at you with those eyes (again?), the same eyes. His lips a grimace of uncertainty.

"Oh nothing. I was just passing by and stopped to rest. That's all. Nothing else. Goodbye."

"Goodbye," you say to him (but you don't say it) and he continues on his way: two ways: your way and my way: way way.

You notice that he's hoarse. Maybe he's got a cold and needs someone to take care of him. Oh Xóchitl, how could you even think of that! He's got his life up the street. You've got yours upstairs on the fifth-floor.

"Will he come back tomorrow?" you ask yourself on the first floor.

"Tomorrow is another day," said the actress at the end of the film. You were struck by her optimism after all she'd suffered: being widowed, leaving her mansion and her bourgeois life, falling in love with the wrong man, seeing her daughter die, fires and diseases, losing her true love (the gallant gentleman leaving the house and subliming into the fog without even saying goodbye, just saying "Frankly, my dear, I don't give a damn," sniff sniff).

On the second floor, you surprise yourself again, thinking about your hair.

On the third, you're surprised at the fear that overtook you when you heard his hoarse voice.

On the fourth floor (those shopping bags—ugh ugh), you're surprised at how you felt when you saw him leaving. What did you want: to run after him and tell him no sweat, that life goes by, then goes by again, and hey, no problem, it's a clean slate —because that's what the readers, our good buddies, expect from you?

Oh Xóchitl! Please!

Surprises and fears.

"They're just the little aftershocks following an earthquake," you reason.

From the fifth-floor, you watch him getting farther away in the half-shadow of the street lights. He walks very sure of himself, ever the conquistador, but at the corner he trips and falls flat on his face. He gets up, brushes off his clothes and continues on his way very sure of himself, ever the conquistador.

Will he come back tomorrow? you ask yourself before going into your apartment.

You can hear the siren of a patrol car coming near—the neighbor ladies were waiting for it.

Tomorrow?
Tomorrow is another day
You go into your pad
you close the door
you wash your hands
you put away the vegetables
you turn on the TV
you take off your shoes
tomorrow
what what
new day
(excuse me?)
it's over the story's over
(are you sure?)
"that's all"
what else
(yes yes no yes yes)
nobody can stop it
(who where what about?)
the inevitable end has arrived/ Farewell
forever, then; farewell forever *butterfly*

163

Here ends
the story
of the bold and virtuous
Conquistador Balboa
and his beloved wife
Florinda
erstwhile called Xóchitl
who roamed
New Spain
of the Deep Blue Sea
and departed from it
for the fearsome
Northernish Empire
in search of
those precious
and famous dollars
that we all know
so well

MCM
XCIV
Playas
de
Tijuana

EPILOGUE

Farewell to the Characters

the moon will forever be a distant love
a mystic incantation of old
that takes your hand, quickly takes hold

—JAVIER ARAIZA

Farewell to the Characters

TIME bequeathed New Spain a long series of viceroys with elegant signatures, as well as an Independence and heroes shot by firing squads, an ephemeral empire, a republic with several dictators, two foreign invasions, the reform laws, an empire with a crazed lady, the Porfirian tyranny, a revolution full of betrayals and murdered heroes, a grade-school teacher with a yen to perpetuate himself, a President-General who wanted to continue his struggle on an island in the Caribbean, useless killings, the Olympics, several monetary devaluations, presidents with elegant signatures, and this book.

Time is an old woman who passes by your house every day offering you bouquets of gardenias. You say to yourself, "Why the hell would I want gardenias when I don't even like flowers?" but sooner or later, you'll buy a bouquet from her and she'll go off happy and not bother you anymore.

Time has left its mark on the characters in this story:

The nurse and the doctor

They got married and are living happily in the Northernish Empire. They no longer work in their fields because their companies were asking for too many qualifications and too much experience. She's a cashier; he's a taxi driver.

167

The bureaucrat conquistadors

Dionisio, Maglorio, Artaldo, Rogaciano, Gaudencio, Carilao, et al, went on with their lives as office workers, earning minimum wage. Some of them thought of going north but it was too far; and out of sight, many of them insist, is out of mind. So it was better to leave well enough alone.

The Marquis del Valle

He died in a small, forgotten house in Castilleja de la Cuesta, a town near Seville. He spent his last nights hoping to receive his just desserts from the king, his lord, and writing letters to dead family members and friends.

The Border of New Spain

It's still there, marking the line that many people have the audacity to cross without proper authorization.

Auachtli

She never found her family, her life never came back, she never again saw the colorful world of her childhood. She spent her last years telling stories of unlucky love affairs. No one knows where she was buried.

The big grouch

Every day is a new adventure, transporting dreamers across New Spain to the mythical Northernish Empire.

Decoroso

He's by himself, looking for happiness.

Onelia

She's by herself, waiting for the return of the Norteño whose face, second by second, grows more and more lost in her memory.

The Norteño

He waited for Onelia as long as he could, until he met Terri (tall, elegant) and married her. He has a daughter named Bianca (like Mick Jagger's ex). He works at a job where you can earn "those precious and famous dollars that we all know so well." His mother is an astrologer. His father-in-law is taller than he is.

Gertrudis and the other girls

Who has not seen them or been enthralled with their splendid beauty? They're still dancing, sharing their private parts with both their regular customers and the tourists. If there's one thing in life that never changes, it's the memory of those girls.

Florinda's mom

She orders the disorder of her drunken husband. She's starting to despise him but she can't admit it.

Florinda's dad

When he's drunk, he still thinks after all these years about the talents of Tonaltlanezi, daughter of aristocrats, never meant for him.

Tonaltlanezi

She shows up a lot in the society pages of the newspapers. They say that money can't buy love but she's bought it several times. They say money can't buy you happiness but she has proved the exception. Her husband is president of an important transnational company and frequently leaves the country to attend conventions that are only an excuse for him to see the disquieting eyes of actress-model Cynthia Madigan. Tonaltlanezi likes bourbon more than any other drink.

Cynthia Madigan

She's happy too. She also likes bourbon best.

La China

After various romantic predicaments, she married a Resident Alien. Currently she is living happily and legally in the Northernish Empire.

Big City Girl

She's in prison for crimes that she insists she didn't commit. Her hatred for chilangos has not diminished, and she often has problems with her cellmates.

Barbie Doll

She's happy as far as anyone knows.

Sufferella

She has everything she needs: understanding children, a loving husband, a savings account. But she clings to sadness like a drunk to the last drops in a bottle.

Hernán Tezozómoc

He realized that Florinda was his true love and he undertook a search for her that lasted for years. He traveled the country, made inquiries and advertised in the papers, desperately seeking Florinda. Frustrated, he returned to the capital, still eager to write his famous *Mexicáyotl Chronicles*, dedicated to his great love.

Fair-haired Mary Ann

She's still working at the restaurant. She's met different men, men who've made her feel pleasure, tenderness or melancholy. She has good memories of all of them.

Balboa's dad and mom

They hardly ever get mail from their long-lost son.

Agents of the Immigration and Naturalization Service
Forgotten by Darwinian theory, they refuse to evolve past their characteristic state of half-man, half-beast. Nevertheless, a famous North American president (with initials RR [or GB or BC?]) gave his assurances that at the End of Time they would stand with the marines, guarding the gates of Paradise. At any rate, someone will come along and break through, out of sheer necessity, and they won't be able to keep him out.

Fat Charlie, the archangel
He retired from his businesses but he still supervises them. His life gets covered in the tabloids. His daughters have renounced him. He's the main character in a song (*Crazy Love*, Vol. II), by that beloved little guy Paul Simon.

The other conquistadors in the Northernish Empire
They want to return to the Mother Country but it's impossible. You see them everywhere (meat cutters, farm workers, mariachis). You never know who they were and they'll never tell you.

Out of Sight
They say it's out of mind, but I can't imagine why.

Author of the letter to Balboa
The authoress still appears in dreams, writing missives to the downtrodden. It's a heavenly gift that few dare exercise.

Professor Spike
A North American filmmaker, his movies take the bull by the horns when it comes to racism and human rights. He's short of stature and bearded. He wears a baseball cap.

The waitresses

They're still unrecognized prophets in matters of the heart.

The boy like all the rest

He advertised in a newspaper: "Seeking young woman (not necessarily young), nice, who likes straightforward conversation and films by Frank Capra."

The mechanics

They put together a rock band and struggled with economic crises and drug problems. Despite this, their most recent hit (*Here She Comes Psst-Psst*) has encouraged them to keep on going with the rock 'n roll gig.

The mustachioed, gray-haired landlord

He tries to seduce girls by reading his poems.

The neighbor ladies

They let you look, they let you admire. They're a Peeping Tom's nirvana.

Oblivion

There it goes, rolling through the world.

Luis Humberto Crosthwaite

Naive writer and neo-hippie, he still believes in peace and love as though they weren't just a nostalgic utopia. He frequently listens to Donovan songs.

In Which the Author Reflects Upon Destiny, Literary Creation and Desserts in Mexico

THE AUTHOR writes the last word of the novel and remembers the title of a song that he includes as a postscript. He attaches the names of the cities in which he writes this interminable-insufferable-diabolical-story-that-he's-lost-so-much-sleep-over, and he includes the dates as a useless point of reference, but finally decides to erase all that because no one gives a shit anyway. He leaves his house running, filled with happiness. He makes two copies and asks for them to be bound. The original, too. He smiles at the girl who's waiting on him (those eyes, that face…could it be you, Ismaelita?). He pays. She says something to him. Something about the novel? He nods without knowing why. He goes home running, filled with happiness. When he checks the coins and bills that the girl gave him, he realizes that she made the change wrong and he's short of money. Lots of money. But it doesn't matter; he's happy even though now he won't be able to afford the quart of milk he needed for his corn flakes. He checks the copies carefully and discovers

173

(oh no) that there's a chapter missing, and—(uh oh) in the original too. It was an important chapter for the story. He runs back, worried. But it's too late now. The girl has left (Ismaelita: gone from my life again?); the door to the store is locked. What was it she said? Did she talk about her childhood, about this novel? The author goes back home, crestfallen. He thinks about destiny. Maybe that chapter never should have been part of the novel. Maybe it was better to take it out and perhaps he should be grateful to the girl. (Ismaelita the intellectual.) Maybe she knew more than he did and that's why she took it out.

"Writing novels isn't a piece of cake," the author muses.

Nobody ever said it was.

Wear your love like heaven.

Luis Humberto Crosthwaite

1. Born in Tijuana, Mexico, on February 28th, 1962.
2. Pisces (so what else is new?).
3. Son of Aurora, also called "La Yoya."
4. Crosses into the United States "legally" since birth.
5. Learned English by watching *The Flintstones* (still doesn't understand why *yabadabadoo* isn't in Webster's).
6. Teresa's husband (thank God).
7. Tall guy with glasses.
8. Father of Santiago and Josue.
9. Jefe at a small press called Yoremito (but who isn't?).
10. Whoever looks into his heart can see the Pacific Ocean—Ah, those beautiful sunsets!
11. Chinese food.
12. Several books.
13. Beer.
14. Artichokes.
15. Did I mention Teresa's big brown eyes?

OTHER CINCO PUNTOS PRESS BOOKS
FROM THE BORDER
& FROM MEXICO

▼

Modelo Antiguo, A Novel of Mexico City
by Luis Eduardo Reyes
(translated by Sharon Franco and Joe Hayes)

The Late Great Mexican Border
Reports from a Disappearing Line
edited by Bobby Byrd and Susannah Mississippi Byrd

Women and Other Aliens
Essays from the U.S./Mexico Border
by Debbie Nathan

Ghost Sickness
poems by Luis Alberto Urrea

Dark and Perfect Angels
poems by Benjamin Alire Sáenz

Eagle-Visioned/Feathered Adobes
poems by Ricardo Sánchez

For more information or a catalog, contact:

CINCO PUNTOS PRESS
2709 Louisville
El Paso, TX 79930
1-800-566-9072